THE YOUNGER MAN

by Dermot Davis

Expression Unleashed Publishing

Most Expression Unleashed Publishing (eXu) print books are available at special quantity bulk purchase discounts for promotional, education or other needs. Additionally, special book excerpts may be created for unique projects. For details, contact the publisher.

———————————————

Expression Unleashed Publishing
Los Angeles, California
http://expressionunleashed.com

ISBN: 0984418156
ISBN-13: 978-0984418152

    Dermot Davis (2014). *The Younger Man*. Expression Unleashed Publishing. Print, 1st Edition.
Printed in the United States of America (or country of purchase).

DEDICATION

For my Parents

CHAPTER 1

Someone once said that nostalgia is longing for a place that you'd never go back to and thinking about it... that's pretty much how I'm feeling about my ex-husband: longing for someone I'd never go back to.

I'm sitting in my favorite café in all of L.A., Café Luna, which is a stone's throw from where my therapist's office is located and from where I've just come. My therapy sessions with Dr. Roberts are usually so intense that I've recently decided to come here afterwards and mull the session over before slotting myself straight back into my mundane life. I just ordered the Eggplant Parmigiana which is usually so smothered in gorgeous parmesan, that I don't have a cheese craving for weeks after, for which my figure thanks me.

I'm sipping a glass of their house Merlot and while soaking in the laid back atmosphere of the restaurant, I also like to people watch. Dating couples usually predominate and tonight is no exception. You can always tell the dating couples: they're the ones that only have eyes for each other and invariably they find each other's conversation entirely riveting. Not that I'm envious, I'm not; but all you have to do is watch how the married couples relate to each other to realize, pretty quick, that the kind of attention that the dating couples give to each other doesn't last.

Married couples tend not to talk so much to each other and when they do, you can tell from their respective responses to each other that what they do have to say isn't that terribly interesting. In fact, when not engaged in conversation, many married couples like to people watch also. Perhaps we are all a tad envious of the dating couples, after all.

I used to love romance and in the early years of my marriage (my second marriage, that is, I don't really count the first one), I was so romanced by my husband that I thought I was the happiest and the luckiest girl alive. I was only a girl. I'm 38 now and that was… 17 years ago, sheesh! I was 21 when Bill swept me off my feet and swore his devoted and undying love to me. I should have gotten him to write that all down and gotten it notarized but I believed him and I guess I foolishly believed that our love would last forever… well for more than ten years, anyway, if that wasn't asking too much.

We did have a marriage contract, after all, so I assumed that that would suffice for a happy-ever-after. At the very least we'd end up taking care of each other in old age, even if by then the glossy sheen of youthful romance had been worn away and faded by life experience. Then again, I have seen enough elderly married couples still doting on each other to keep my hopes up that romance can still exist and last into our autumn years.

"More wine?" the polite twenty-something handsome waiter asks with a smile. With wavy hair and soft brown eyes, he looks like he's new as I haven't noticed him working here before.

"Sure," I answer and he reads my mind and tells me that my Eggplant Parmigiana is, "on its way." Nearly every waiter in Los Angeles is an aspiring actor, writer or director and judging from the new guy's good looks, I'm guessing actor.

Sometimes it's hard to tell if I'm reading the situation right or not but I do seem to get a lot of interest from guys over fifty and guys in their twenties especially. I'm not sure why that is. Well, sure, guys over fifty years of age I can understand, I'm considered a youngster by them, but what's with the young guys checking out an older chick like me?

"Your wine," the waiter says, returning to my table and giving me a million-dollar smile.

"Thank you," I say, only mildly returning his enthusiasm for fear of encouraging him to engage in small talk. After a brief awkward moment, off he goes. I'm probably imagining it so I make a point to watch how he treats his other tables and see what grade of smile he greets them with. Maybe he thinks I'm an agent or someone who could help his career along. I make a point of not checking out his cute, tight ass as he totters off.

I'm so done with men.

I smile to myself remembering Dr. Roberts' poker-faced look, the one that she gives to me when I say that to her. "Why do you say that?" she asks me, unable to prevent one of her classic raised eyebrow looks.

"I don't know where to begin," I tell her, thinking of a laundry list of reasons.

"Start anywhere," she says.

"Well… first of all I don't miss the… heartache," I say, choosing my words carefully. "I've been without a man for almost three years and… I like being single," I tell her.

"You *like* being single or perhaps you believe it to be the lesser of two evils?" she asks.

I had to think hard before I answered because Dr. Roberts can make me squirm like no other and has a knack for making me eat my badly chosen words. "I guess what I mean is I've given up on love," I say and then have to clarify. "I've given up on getting the love that I want… from men."

"You've given up on romantic love," she says, seeking clarification.

"Yes," I ponder and then answer. "I've given up thinking that romantic love... is a viable... that romantic love lasts. Actually, scratch that. Romantic love is a crock," I add, my emotions rising, "It's a huge hoax... a fairytale. Romantic love is a pile of..."

"Shit?" Dr. Roberts asks when I don't finish my emphatic sentence.

"Yeah," I answer. "Romantic love is a huge pile of shit."

Dr. Roberts sits back in her chair and kinda nods her head, which usually means that she thinks I've come to some sort of epiphany or conclusion in my thinking and as she usually does, she then remains quiet, expecting me to talk some more about my eventual realization.

Hearing those words come out of my mouth like that is pretty shocking to me, actually. I've believed in romantic love all my life and in some respects, for many years it was my reason for getting up in the morning. I used to think that, apart from romantic love, what else was there in life? I mean, sure you can have a career; you can have hobbies and interests; you can even have a family and kids... but if you didn't truly have love from your man... what was the point?

"Eggplant Parmigiana," the waiter says and smiles as he places the steaming hot dish before me. "Can I get you anything else?" he asks, his adorable brown eyes looking more deeply into mine than the eyes of an anonymous food server should.

"No, this is... this looks terrific," I say, not joking, as I look lustfully at my food. I cannot wait to sink my teeth into this gorgeous dish and in truth, this yummy eggplant and cheese is the only thing I have eyes for right now.

"Enjoy," he says and seems reluctant to leave; or perhaps it's totally my imagination, which wouldn't be the first time for me. I feel like I've been married for so long, I don't know what it's like to be hit on in public. If I was here with Bill, the waiter wouldn't have given me a second thought. For some reason, a single woman dining alone is some kind of curiosity to a lot of people; I can almost see the other diners looking at me and wondering, "Hmm, a woman eating alone... I wonder what her story is. Has she been stood up?"

Just as I'm about to dig into my yummy dish, I get a text from my friend and work colleague, Ronald. "Have the plans for the theater piece. Swing by later?"

Ronald is a film and TV production designer and has been subcontracting work out to me since I got divorced and needed to find some employment for myself. Over the years, he's become a good friend and for some reason, likes to confide in me and seek my advice about his romances. It's like he thinks I'm some kind of expert. At this stage, I know exactly what his text implies. When he wants to swing by my place at night or at the weekends, it usually means that he's having some love trouble and needs my objective opinion.

"Sure, come on by after 8. ☐," I text back.

As I finally gorge on the hot eggplant and cheese, I look around at the courting couples and, in truth, I almost pity them. Sure, it's all smiles and best impressions now but just wait till you really get to know each other, I feel like telling them.

When we were dating, eons ago at this stage, Bill used to look at me like I was the only thing that existed in all of reality. His attention and outright devotion to me was utterly intoxicating and I was totally swept off my feet. "You are my world," he'd say, with that totally besotted look of his. "My heart belongs to you and you only," he told me more than once.

When he met me I was married, I had a young kid and I kept giving him the brush off, yet still he persisted. He bought me gifts, many of which I returned as inappropriate and despite my lack of reciprocity, he practically stalked me. He did not take no for an answer and I guess, with such unwavering persistence, he wore me down till I finally said yes.

He didn't care that I was married and in truth, it wasn't a happy marriage of two compatible people, quite the opposite. But still... what kind of guy relentlessly pursues a married woman? I may have been young but I should have known better: once a cheater, always a cheater.

Not that I can talk; cheating on Steve wasn't my greatest moment. We may not have been compatible and even though I was secretly miserable, Steve didn't deserve to be cheated upon. There are more noble ways to exit a mismatched coupling than sneaking off to meet a lover in anonymous hotel rooms. Of course, at the time, our illicit meetings were thrilling and absolutely exhilarating. Talk about fireworks. The earth-shattering, mind-blowing connection that I had with Bill was... well, let's just say that I lost my head as well as my heart. At the time I couldn't fathom a life being apart from him: which makes his loss almost fifteen years later almost... unbearable.

"How are we doing here?" the waiter asks and manages to catch me with a mouthful of hot cheese. Nodding my head wildly to denote complete satisfaction, he still doesn't leave. "Good, huh?" he asks, beginning to nod his own head, as if he's talking to a child or an old person with dementia. "Let me know if you need anything," he then says and again I nod, as if to say, "sure thing, now please leave." Finally, he does.

Bill and I used to come here a lot, actually, the fact of which seemed to surprise Dr. Roberts. "Most people exhibiting your degree of heartbreak would tend to stay away from places that they used to share with their ex, for fear that they would bring up unhappy memories," she had said carefully.

Maybe my decision to come back here is an unconscious desire to stay connected to those happier moments, I don't know. I don't hate Bill. We shared some absolutely amazing and fabulous years together and when his attention was focused upon me, it was... magical and wonderful and life-sustaining. Ever since I met him, it was almost as if his attention made me feel alive; as if for the first time I existed to myself; as if I finally became a real person. Being seen by him made me feel like I belonged in this world.

When he stopped looking at me and directed his attention elsewhere... it was like I had died; as if I became invisible; invisible to myself, just as much as if I became too small to see in the greater world. It felt like my soul had drifted down into a dark, dark void... and I've yet to come back up and fully reclaim myself.

"Coffee or dessert?" the waiter asks as he signals to inquire if I'm finished with the half uneaten plate of food before me that I've suddenly lost all appetite for.

"No thanks," I answer.

"Will I put this in a box to go?" he asks helpfully.

"Yes, please," I say, thinking to myself that it would make a good breakfast.

"Do you go there thinking that... hoping that maybe Bill will magically show up and come running into your arms, tell you how much that he can't live without you and insist that his affair was just a big mistake? That it's you and it's always been you?" Dr. Roberts asks.

"No, of course not," I answer, lying to her and to myself.

"In case I didn't tell you the first time, my name is John and it's been a delight to wait on you this evening," the waiter says, a glint in his dark eyes as he places the "to go" container on the table.

"Thank you... John," I say. "It was... lovely."

When I get back to my apartment, Ronald has already arrived and was waiting patiently for me.

"Are you here a long time?" I ask him.

"No, just arrived," he says, knowing that he's early and I'm not late. "I hope I didn't rush you."

"Not at all, Ronald," I answer, opening the door. "Did you eat?" I ask him, willing to give up my eggplant if the poor guy is starving.

"I'm really not hungry," he answers. "But thanks."

"Is everything okay?" I ask as I switch on the lights in the apartment.

"Yeah," he answers unconvincingly. "I've got the plans for the Taper play," he says as he unfolds some preliminary sketches. "They're not sure what they want exactly so they're open to input. It's a non-realistic setting and kind of... experimental," he says, his voice faltering.

"What's going on?" I ask, touching his shoulder to comfort him.

"Oh, it's this long distance thing... it's not working," he confides. "I think he might be cheating on me."

"What makes you think that?"

"I don't know for sure. It's just the way he talks sometimes."

"Did you ask him straight out?" I ask.

"Yes, several times but he gets upset and tells me that I'm paranoid and... insecure. Of course I'm insecure, everybody's insecure... who isn't insecure?" he asks. "Besides, he's done nothing to make me feel secure in this relationship and telling me that I'm insecure does not make me feel any less insecure... right?"

"That's right," I agree. "Want something to drink? I was going to make some coffee, want some?"

"Sure," he says. "Do you have decaf?"

Looking almost teary and vulnerable, Ronald follows me into the kitchen as I prepare some hot water to make the coffee.

"I'm sorry," he says. "I don't want to lay all this on you. I just get so... this long distance thing is driving me crazy."

"What's the chances of either of you...?"

"I need to be here for work and he needs to be up there for the same reason so we're kinda... screwed, as far as a long term thing is concerned," he says, anticipating my question. "I love San Francisco but I couldn't just pack up everything I've built up here for so long, over so many years. Maybe it's just not meant to be."

"Are you okay with that?" I ask.

"Well, we have to give it a try first, right? I mean we can't just throw in the towel at the first bump in the... it's still early days, don't you think?"

"Yeah, of course," I say, not really knowing what to say. "You have to give it your best shot. At least then you can say that you tried everything."

"Exactly," he agrees, as if that's precisely what he really wanted to hear. "No one loves a quitter."

"There's cream in the fridge," I tell him as my phone rings. "I need to get this, do you mind? It's Janice."

"No, of course not," he says, slapping the air with his hand.

"Hi, Janice," I answer the call.

"Aunt Doris wants to know what my situation is," she says, forsaking any greeting, as usual.

"Your situation about what?" I ask her.

"Gram's birthday party. She wants to know how many people are going to crash at her place."

"Yeah?" I ask, still not knowing what the purpose of her call is.

"I have so much work to do and a deadline for my short to hand in... do I really have to go?" she asks, finally.

"No, of course you don't have to go. It's a big birthday for my mom and I know that she'd love it if everyone was there to share it with her but if you're too busy..."

"See, you always do this," Janice interrupts. "You always guilt trip me into doing everything that you want."

"I'm sorry if that's how it sounds but your grammy adores you and she'd be..."

"Fine," Janice interrupts. "How am I going to get there? I can't afford the gas for my POS jeep and I don't think it'll make it anyway..."

"Are you bringing your friend?" I ask.

"My 'friend'?" Janice scoffs. "Her name is Jane. And no, why would I ask her to come along? It's totally not... her scene."

"You can come with me. I'll come pick you up," I suggest. There's a silence as Janice seems to be thinking it over.

"You're not going to be playing those books on tapes are you? All that self-improvement bullshit stuff?"

I can feel my jaw stiffen as I try to stay calm and control my temper. No one pushes my buttons quite like my twenty-year-old daughter and lately that's all she seems to want to do, as if she's secretly getting some kind of thrill out of it.

"No, I don't have to play anything on the drive up. We can talk all the way," I say to her, knowing that she'll consider that worse than any books on tape that I might play.

"I'll bring some stuff we can play. I've been listening to some really good stuff lately; I think that you'll really like it," she says, her tone softening.

"We don't have to decide that now," I tell her. "I'm just glad that you've decided to come celebrate with your grammy. I know she's going to be totally excited."

"Yeah," she says. "Gotta go."

"It's your mom's birthday?" Ronald asks when I hang up from Janice.

"Yeah, she's turning seventy in a couple of weeks," I answer.

"Cool," Ronald says distractedly, as he takes a sip of his hot coffee.

CHAPTER 2

I don't know if I really expect Bill to come running back into my arms but I will admit that a scenario like that has been a fantasy of mine, even if that daydream has been slowly fading in intensity as time moves on. Truthfully, I don't think I would actually ever take him back, even if he did return with his tail between his legs and a heartfelt, sincere apology on his lips. There's been too much deep hurt on my part and, seriously, I don't think my heart would be up for it. I just don't have the amount of hope left in my reserves that it would take to bounce back from my intense heartbreak.

It's another beautiful sunny day in LA as I drive through Santa Monica on my way to meet Steve for lunch. I love my beemer. If getting a divorce from Bill had any silver linings it was getting a really nice pay day and years of alimony for my trouble. I love California divorce laws; not sure I would have done so well in Mississippi or some other state.

"Hey, Steve," I say as I greet him with a kiss on the cheek. "Have you been here long?" I ask as he looks so casual and at ease, sitting at a table outside the trendy Westside hipster cafe. Steve loves all the LA hipster places. He's like a teenager trapped inside the body of a middle-aged man; which is exactly why it never worked with us, but that's another story.

"Just arrived, sweetheart. No worries. You're looking fantastic today!" he says as he gets up to hold out a chair for me, always the gentleman.

"Thanks," I say, settling in.

"I mean it," he insists, as if I took his compliment

too casually. "You don't age. What's your secret?"

"I don't know. Good genes?"

"That can't be it. I've met your sister," he says. "Not that she's old looking; she looks her age, I guess. She could maybe get some work done; last time I saw her, her neck was looking kinda..."

"Steve, I'm not here to talk about Doris," I interrupt, opening up the menu. Steve is one of those people that, although he has a heart of gold, can act and talk like a complete jerk sometimes. It is as if there's a complete disconnect between his private and public persona. I've never understood the psychology but it probably has to do with people that have sensitive souls feeling as if they have to talk and act tough as some kind of a defense mechanism. Having said that, for people that don't know him like I do, Steve can come across like a total jackass.

"What are you hungry for?" he asks as I check out the vegetarian options.

"Something light," I answer. "Anything that doesn't have cheese in it. Just a salad, I guess."

"I thought that you like cheese?" he asks.

"I love cheese. It just has a habit of travelling straight from my stomach to my thighs."

"How's that daughter of yours?" he asks. "Breaking hearts, as usual?"

I want to answer that the only heart that she's been breaking lately is mine but I don't particularly want to go there with Steve. "She's doing well, I guess. Since she started college, I don't see her as much as I would like."

"Well, she's at that age, isn't she? Once guys come on the scene, they've no time for anybody else," he says sagely.

"I wish that was it," I answer. "I kinda wish she was with a nice boy that she was crazy about."

"She's not dating anybody?" he asks with surprise, verging on shock. "She's gorgeous," he adds.

"She *is* dating," I clarify. "She's dating... she just seems to be going through some phase at the moment, questioning her sexuality... experimenting or something."

Steve looks at me for a long moment, probably trying to decode my ramblings. "She's into chicks?" he asks, his eyebrows raised so high on his forehead that they look comical.

"She *is* seeing someone and apparently her name is Jane," I say, sounding weary as if I don't want to have this conversation, which I don't.

"Wow," he says, genuinely shocked. "She's such a looker."

"What's that got to do with it?" I ask, equally shocked.

"I'm just saying," he says, saying nothing.

"You're just saying what? That pretty women should only date guys?"

"But she used to date guys, right? I mean, this is... I guess I'm not understanding," he says, his head looking strained from his mental exertions.

"You and me both," I concur. "She dated guy after guy until she moved into that place in Venice beach. Whatever crowd she's hanging out with now..." I say, not sure exactly how to finish my thought.

"Venice beach is wild," Steve says. "I mean, everyone knows that that place is a zoo, full of freaks. The whole place is one big freak show," Steve says, as if he's trying to console me or something, which he isn't. "She'll grow out of it; it's just a phase. A pretty girl like her."

"What's her being pretty got to do with it?" I almost yell. "What are you saying? That only ugly women are lesbians?"

Taken aback at my mini outburst, Steve seems to stop and think about what he really is thinking; as if, internally, he might actually be owning up to some false belief on his part. "You think she's a lesbian?" he asks, hushing down the last word of the question.

"I don't know. Like I say, I think it might be some kind of phase. She's opted for feminist studies in her course work; feminist filmmakers through the ages or some such bullshit..." I say, suddenly feeling exhausted.

"Wow," Steve says, returning to look at the menu upon seeing the waiter approach. "What about you?" he asks, once we give our orders and the waiter rambles off. "Are you seeing anyone?"

"No, I'm not seeing anyone," I answer, as if it's one of the most ridiculous questions I ever heard. "You know that I'm sworn off dating... and don't you dare begin your next question with, 'a pretty woman like you,' or I swear I'll stab you with your steak knife," I threaten, only half joking.

"You haven't met anyone that you're attracted to? Nobody at all has caught your eye?" he persists.

Even though I had an instant rebuttal at the ready, I actually got a surprise when John the waiter suddenly shot into my mind. I had an instant image of him leaning towards me with his million dollar smile and his matinee idol good looks. "No, I'm not considering... there's nobody that... I'm done with men," I blubber unconvincingly.

"Yes, there is," he says, squinting at me. "Who is it? Someone you met at your work?"

"No, really, there is nobody. Just some guy I think was kinda crushing on me. I don't know him; it was at a restaurant."

"Did you give him your—" he asks and I hurriedly interrupt.

"No, I didn't give him anything, Steve. He was a

young kid who probably hits on anyone cute in a skirt."

"A kid? Like, how old?"

"I don't know, twenties. What would a twenty-something-year-old guy be interested in... someone like me, anyway? I don't get it."

"That's because you don't know what women that age are like. Girls his age can be, I don't know, spoilt little bitches. All they seem to care about are clothes, cars, money and celebrities. Of course a young guy would be digging you; they hate that shit."

"Isn't Stacy that age?" I ask, referring to his girlfriend.

"Yeah, but she's not like that. Even if she was, I'd still date her; she's hot."

"You're such a... Neanderthal, you know that?" I tell him, masking a grin with my glass of water.

"You should take him out for a ride some day, get that fire burning again before it goes out altogether. Doesn't have to be anything serious, in fact... best thing if it's not something serious. Go have a wild fling, why don't you?"

"I told you, Steve and I'm serious... and thanks to you, this conversation has confirmed my resolve, even more: I'm done with men."

"A pretty woman like you," he says with a huge smirk as he takes up his steak knife and holds it away from the table.

"You're such an asshole," I say and despite my best efforts, a smile breaks out on my face.

Feeling victorious, a broad smile breaks out on Steve's face too. "You know, if I wasn't dating Stacy, you could have been in with a shot," he says.

"Don't push it, Steve," I say, picking up my fork in jest. "How *are* things going with you two?"

"Terrific!" he says, smiling like he really means it. "She's like, almost half my age; I'm a very lucky old man. I don't know what she sees in me, either. She tells all the time that she's happy... so who am I to argue?"

"That's wonderful... really," I say, genuinely feeling happy for him. "You deserve it and thank heavens some people in my world are having a successful relationship. You give me and the rest of the world hope," I say, raising my glass in a toast.

On the drive back home I get a call from Ronald so I put him on speakerphone. "Have you come up with any designs yet?" he asks.

"I've got some ideas but to be perfectly honest, I've no idea what the concept is," I answer.

"I don't think they're quite sure themselves which is why they told me that they're wide open for suggestions. Did you read the play I emailed you?"

"Yeah. Most of it."

"What did you think?" he asks and I hesitate before I answer.

"I don't really understand it. I know that it's avant garde or whatever but is the first act set in a... in someone's dialogue they mention purgatory, right... and the second act is set in a hell of some kind?"

"Yeah, that's what I got," he agrees. "So we need something that can suggest both emotional spaces without hitting it too much on the nose..."

"No fire and brimstone..."

"Exactly. Look, I know it's not the cleanest of assignments but just draw up some ideas and we can present them to get their feedback, maybe get some greater clarity as to what they really want, okay?"

"I can do that," I say. "I'll work on it today and

maybe get something back to you this evening or tomorrow early."

"Perfect," Ronald says and I wait to hear if he has anything more to say, which he doesn't. "Talk to you later, then," I say and hang up.

Putting on a pot of coffee, I make myself comfortable on my sofa and open up the stage play on my tablet to see if I can get some better idea of what the darn thing is really about and maybe see if I can get some images from the text that would help in suggesting some meaningful stage design. It's a modern translation of some obscure French play which was originally written in the last century... and boy, is it bleak.

I hate plays whose meaning is so buried in sub-text that you have no idea what's going on half the time and you have to rely on the theater playbill notes to be guided as to the real meaning. Unfortunately for me there are no program notes to help and the play is so obscure, nothing helpful comes up on any of the internet search engines.

From what I can gather, there's these group of people who have died and are in some state of purgatory. Therese, the lead character has to sort out her differences among them that she didn't sort out on earth before she can move on. If she can resolve her relationships successfully, she can go to what seems to be a kind of heaven, where everything is all bright and beautiful. That's not the case, of course, and sure enough she finds herself in some dark and horrible place, which is depressing as, well... hell.

What's supposed to be different about the play is the fact that the lead character is a woman, which, according to a Wiki entry on the web, was a radical departure for theater in France at that time. I don't see why

24

that little nugget would have any relevance for today as having a female lead character in a play is hardly going to shock LA theater-goers... unless there's some kind of strip-tease involved and actually, even then, that's no biggie anymore.

The more I read the darn thing, the sadder I become. The main character, Therese, has so many unresolved issues with her husband and her lover and her daughters that I'm finding it really hard to detach myself from her predicament. As much as I try to disengage, I find that I'm comparing myself to her plight. Will I end up in some dark and depressing hellhole if I don't resolve all of the issues in my relationships?

Falling into a pit of despair I put the play aside and put on some music that I know will cheer me up; one of my all time classic go-to bands for shifting my bad mood: the Beach Boys. Playing it loud, I stand up, sing as best I can and move my body to the happy vibes. It doesn't work.

After ten minutes of forced cheerfulness, not only is my bad mood not shifting but it seems to be getting worse. My heart is beating like crazy and something in me feels like it's screaming its friggin' head off and wants nothing more than to jump off the nearest tall building; so I turn off the music, grab my phone and call Dr. Roberts to see if she can fit me in for later in the day. Luckily for me she does have a cancellation and just knowing that I'm going to see her in a short while calms me right down. Jeez, I'm a mess, I almost say aloud.

CHAPTER 3

"Going back on anti-depressants isn't a sign of failure or regression," Dr. Roberts says as I sit across from her in a much calmer state that I had been earlier.

"I know. I just… I want to be with my feelings, rather than… I'd prefer to feel pain… than to feel numb all the time. I know I'm going to have bad days," I say, half regretting that I'd called her office in such a trigger-happy, off-the-cuff moment. "I think because I've slacked off on what was working for me, the yoga, for instance, I'm not handling things as well. I need to get back into a routine and not blow it off so much. I haven't been to a group therapy workshop in a while… I need to get back to… I guess, I just felt like I was more healed than I really am."

"How are you feeling at this moment?"

"Fine. Much better, thank you. I think I just panicked."

"You did right to call."

"Thank you," I say, happier for her saying that.

"Most people would have poured themselves a large whisky or something."

"I guess."

"So, what brought it on? You were reading a book?"

"It's a play, for work. I'm supposed to be designing a set."

"Where does it take place?" Dr. Roberts asks and I instantly smile.

"In hell," I answer. I don't know why I'm smiling and I know right away that that's going to be her next question.

"Why does that make you smile?" she asks and I

smile even more, almost breaking into a giggle.

"I guess, I don't think of... hell, too often. It just seems like, I don't know... funny."

"Is it funny because it's too bleak to even contemplate, perhaps?" she asks soberly.

"I don't think I even believe in a hell," I say, confused about the whole subject. "I don't know why I find it funny. It just is." Dr. Roberts stays purposefully quiet which is always her way of getting me to talk more. "The character in the play is a female and she has all these relationships that went to shit and if she doesn't resolve them... she's going to hell... basically," I say and then stay quiet letting her know that I'm not going to say anything more.

"I see," she says and I can almost hear her mental wheels turning. "So you feel that if you don't resolve your relationships... you'll suffer the same fate?"

"I guess sometimes I think I've made such a mess of everything... like all the people in my life... hate me..." I say and begin to cry.

"Do you believe that to be true?" Dr. Roberts asks as she passes me a box of tissues. "That everybody in your life hates you?"

"No, I don't believe it to be true... and if they do, I don't blame them. I've made some pretty shitty decisions... oh, I don't know," I say wearily, realizing that we've both been here before and that I seem to be going around in circles. I've been coming here for years; maybe this whole therapy thing isn't working and I'm just blowing a whole bunch of money for nothing.

"I feel like I'm in a rut," I blurt out. "I'm bored with my life and I don't have anything... there's nothing for me to look forward to. It's just the same old shit everyday and I hate it."

Dr. Roberts does her sit back in her chair thing, as if she thinks we're getting somewhere and I'm sure that she's loving this therapy moment but I'm not feeling it and I really just want to run out and get on with my life. I blow my nose loudly.

"I sense some anger," she says.

"If I'm angry it's because of all the shitty mistakes I've made and I can't get them back; I can't get my life back. I'm nearly forty years old, jeez, and... my life wasn't supposed to be like this. I had no idea it was going to turn out so... fucked up."

"You think that you're life is messed up beyond repair?"

"It's not about 'repair,'" I say angrily. "It's like gone, done... it's like someone wave me a magic wand and give me a do-over. I don't want to be a washed-up angry forty-year-old, unmarried and unloved... spinster. I don't have a home and a family... and a dog. It wasn't supposed to... how did I... " I don't know what I'm saying anymore so I stop babbling and take another tissue from the box.

"Suppose someone did give you a magic wand that could erase the mistakes you've made in the past. Which one would be first on your list... off the top of your head?"

"I would have said no to Bill," I immediately say. "I would have run a million miles from him and shielded my eyes that very first time he looked into mine. That's the look I always remember... that's the look that never goes away."

When I leave Dr. Roberts' office I drive straight to Café Luna and it isn't until I'm parked outside that I wonder how I got here. Am I really going into the restaurant again for like the third time this week? Thinking about what my alternatives are, I realize that I really don't have much going on. Going home to a lonely and empty apartment doesn't seem all that attractive.

Maybe I'll kill a few hours here and when I get home, it'll be early to bed. There is no way I am going to attempt working on that lousy play until the morning at least. I decide then and there to do two hours of yoga and meditation, first thing in the morning, before I even start thinking about the project.

As I try to do the best that I can to fix my face, after a tearful session with Dr. Roberts, I suddenly panic that I might actually see John the waiter again. Maybe it's a mixture of excitement and panic because secretly a part of me is thinking that, if he's working tonight, his inevitable flirting might cheer me up and make me feel like I'm still a desirable female, after all. I'm so full of contradictions that I wonder does everyone feel the way I do or is it just me?

Everyone else just seems to know what they want and what makes them happy and seem to live their lives with much more certainty than I ever could. My sister Doris dated around for a while but then, when she finally tired of the dating scene, she decided it was time for her to get married; so she found a suitable guy on the internet who was also ready to settle down; they got married, bought a house and now it's happily ever after for them both.

What would my life have been like if I hadn't gotten pregnant at eighteen? I'd be such a perfect speaker to go visit schools to tell teenagers not to have sex until they get married. Seriously. Even though I'm still not happy with my post tearful, puffy eyes, I take a few deep breaths and am able to rouse myself from the cushy safety of my beemer.

"Is that you, Frances?" a male voice asks. It takes me a few moments to recognize the guy but I'm still not sure where I know him from. "Vernon," he then says, "I worked with you on a few installations... I used to do moldings... the Pacific Design Center?"

"Oh, that's right," I then remember, "how are you doing?"

It's funny how sometimes people seem to remember me so well but I barely remember them; it's as if I loomed large in their lives but they played but a bit role in mine. Of course, it works the other way around too, so it's just human nature, I guess. I do remember now that Vernon was someone that had a definite crush on me and like all men that felt that way with me when I was married, I never truly befriended him. The way that he's looking at me now reminds me of his past romantic attachment so I'm not going to act too chummy with him now, either.

"Are you still doing the interior decorating?" he asks.

"No, not anymore. Production design," I say, hoping to be excused.

"You still look great," he says, his eyes burning hotly into me.

"Thanks, so do you."

"You look happy," he says, as if he's surprised. Did I not look happy then, I wonder? "Are you still with your boyfriend?" he asks and I don't correct him and say that who he is referring to was my husband; unless, of course, he's got me totally confused with someone else.

"Why do you ask?" I say, feeling a bit peeved and maybe a little bold. "Why do you ask that question? About my boyfriend."

"I'm sorry," he apologizes, "I don't want to seem rude. It's just that you always seemed, I don't know... it was like you only seemed happy if your boyfriend was happy and if he was sad... you were sad. I'm not speaking out of line, am I?"

"No, not at all," I say, lying like crazy. Who is this guy that I barely even know? I feel like telling him to go fly a kite or something but I don't and yet I still manage to smile. "Well, take care now. Nice to bump into you," I say and move along, not even caring if he's done with the conversation or not. What a friggin' nerve.

My mood shifts immediately when I walk into the safe confines of the restaurant and the soft lights and plush surroundings works its magic. I feel calm again. The young hostess doesn't flinch when I say, "Table for one," and she takes me to the same table where I was seated the last few times. Is this their table which is reserved for solo diners, I wonder?

The soft music soothes my nerves and I peruse the menu. I feel like having the eggplant parm again but I dare not get it twice in one week. What did that guy mean about me being happy only if the man I was with was happy? That I'm not my own person independent of the man I'm in relationship with? Is that true? I'm feeling pretty shocked when I think that I've spent most of my life in a relationship with one man or another.

I began dating as soon as boys began paying attention to me which was very early on because I was considered a "looker" at a very young age. I'm beginning to think now that being fortunate with good looks is not the blessing that I always thought that it was. It's only for the past three years that I've really been alone and two of those I can write off straight away as I only made it through them because I was in an anti-depressant haze and spent my non-work time curled up in bed either crying or reading serial romances…. after which I'd then cry all over again.

I don't know… it's all so confusing. If the past year is what being single and independent is all about, I'd rather choose relationship because being alone all the time sucks. I'm sick of being with myself and having nothing to do except think and talk to myself about thinking and then thinking some more.

I've been seeing Dr. Roberts for so long that, at this point, I actually carry her around in my head everywhere I go. How do you feel about that? What do you mean when you say such-and-such, I can hear her voice inquire within my head. I now know why people drink and do drugs: it's to shut out the internal chitter-chatter which, in my case, is going to drive me insane some day. I talk to myself so much that I'm beginning to hate my own company.

"What can I start you off with?" John the waiter stands before me and gives me that million dollar smile, which tonight looks like it just got a raise to a billion dollars. There are those sexy brown eyes of his, looking at me as if he's undressing me even as he stands there in his silky black shirt and cute tight black pants looking innocent, like butter wouldn't melt in that sensuous, sultry mouth of his; a half smirk on his face makes him look like he knows secrets that no one else knows.

"A glass of the house merlot?" he asks with familiarity, like he's letting me know that he knows what my beverage of choice is and as if to flatter me.

"I think I'll go with the cabernet," I tell him, letting him know that I'm not going to be one of his conquests, or yet another addition to his many groupies, thank you very much.

"Very good," he says, smiling as if he's about to lick his lips and is readying himself up for the challenge. I'm positive that he's thinking that the only reason I'm here, yet again, is to see him. Oh, heavens, why on earth did I come in here tonight?

Maybe I *should* just throw all caution to the wind and have a wild fling; if everybody's cards are on the table, who can it hurt? I've often wondered to myself if, by having some short-term romances, it might help me forget Bill sooner, like exorcising his memories by replacing them with something else; some other memories less hurtful. By not having sex, since Bill left, it's almost like he still has a hold over my body, almost like it was his alone and no other man should come along and...

"Cabernet," John the waiter interrupts my thoughts by placing what looks like an extra large glass of red wine before me. I look askance at the glass of wine before looking at his barely-contained grinning face as if to let him know that I know that that is not the regular size glass of wine. He adopts an exaggerated straight face, as if he's playing some private game with me. "Are you ready to place your order?" he asks.

"Not yet," I reply, as cool and as impartially as I can manage. "Give me a few more minutes."

"Take your time," he says and I could swear that he gave me the smallest wink just as he was leaving. As he turns, this time, I do check out his cute little bum which, in those tight little pants of his, sends a little quiver from my heart to my tippy toes.

Jeez, what is wrong with me? My flesh is all goose bumps and I know that I'm just a glass of wine away from feeling and acting like a horny little schoolgirl, if I really allowed myself the indulgence.

Is this what years and years without sex does to the body? As if I didn't have enough conflicting voices in my head, I have to deal with raging hormones and a body that's so hungry for human touch that it shivers at the mere sight of a cute ass? Somebody please save me from myself.

Okay, not that I'm really contemplating this, I mean let's just say, as a fantasy, that I put myself out there and gave the guy my phone number; is he seriously interested? What if I'm just imagining the whole thing and he's like this with everybody? Closing my menu, as if I'm ready to order, I look innocently around to see exactly where he is in the restaurant.

I turn and see him at a far table taking a young couple's order. I don't see any smiles or winks and the way that he's standing at the table is so different than the way he stood at mine; his body is angled away from them, whereas he stood totally facing me, like he could have hugged me if I stood up.

As if he can feel my eyes searing into his hot body, he turns and immediately looking over at me, he smiles and mouths, "Be right there." I smile back and nod but then I realize that a young guy sitting at a table with his date thinks I'm smiling at him and he gives me a big smile. Instantly embarrassed, I turn my head back around and open up the menu.

Okay, I'm not imagining it. John the waiter is definitely flirting with me; which makes me feel terrified and excited all at the same time. Now what?

Before I talk myself out of it, which I know I'm very well capable of doing, I take out my business card and slip it into the menu so that when he takes my order... no, what am I doing?

"Sorry about that," John the waiter says, looking totally delighted to be back at my table. "What can I get you?"

"I'm going to have the Caesar salad," I say, "and can you bring some more bread?"

"Sure thing," he says and I watch him take the menu away, with my business card attached to the paperclip that holds the slip of paper advertizing the nights' specials.

As I watch him vanish into the kitchen, my earlier feeling of excitement has now been totally replaced with its opposite nemesis: full-on total dread. Feeling absolutely terrified, I have the sudden urge to leave some money on the table and scamper the hell out of there before he returns from the kitchen with a knowing wink and a smile, having now been given power over me by silly ol' me declaring my hand before he does. I don't even know what his intentions are; he's going to think I'm some cougar or something, out on the prowl.

Frantically searching through my purse, I can't believe that I haven't brought any cash with me. The fact that I seldom carry cash is irrelevant; I feel like I'm totally screwed. That look and that smile? It's just like Bill all over again; why didn't I see the resemblance sooner? Not that he looks like Bill; it's just his energy and his cool hand Luke attitude and that practiced smile that exists for one purpose and one purpose only: to seduce and steal some hearts. Well, that's two purposes, I know...

Just as I'm having a mini meltdown, a dating couple at an adjoining table is having some kind of argument. Standing up, looking outraged, this poor guy's date is going ballistic: I think she just called him a schizophrenic moron or something and now she's storming off. This is the same guy that thought I was smiling at him earlier and he's now looking at me with the saddest puppy dog eyes.

I smile to cheer him up and he mouths something to me that sounds like, "I'll never get a maid." I have seen him here before with different women: has he been interviewing for a maid? Sure looked like serial dating to me. "I guess this is your table, huh?" he says to me as he confidently strolls over, drink in hand.

"Creature of habit, I guess," I answer.

"Do you always eat alone?" he asks.

"No. I used to do what you're doing," I say, a mischievous smile breaking out on my face that I'm not quite sure where it came from.

"Touché," he says, smiling and I can tell that he's digging me. "What's your name?"

"Frances."

"Martin," he says, extending his hand, which I automatically shake. "Mind if I join you?" he asks.

"Please do," I say and I'm truly glad for the company. As he sits down, I actually feel a wave of relief run through my body. Not knowing how I was going to last the rest of my meal having put myself out there with John the waiter, I really wasn't sure if I could survive the humiliation of fancy-pants John, looking at me with a knowing smirk on his face, for the remainder of the evening.

As this young man magically appears from nowhere, I kinda take it as a sign that taking it any further with John the waiter is not such a good idea; in fact, I know right to my bones that it's not a good idea. This goofy-looking kid doesn't know it but he probably saved me from myself and prevented me from making yet another excursion down humiliation lane. Maybe someone is looking out for me, after all.

"How's the dating going?" I ask him with interest. I'm actually relishing the idea of talking to someone I don't know; someone that doesn't know me and my history and doesn't look at me like I'm an emotional basket case, like most of the people I know do... and I know they do, whether they have the guts to admit it to me or not.

Having been out of the dating scene for so long, I'm kind of curious to hear it from someone that's so obviously in the front line, finding out first hand from someone in the dating scene trenches, so to speak.

"Not so good," he admits and I must say, his honesty is refreshing. You think John the waiter would be so honest? I don't think so. Our food is placed before us by what seems now to be a surly waiter. I look up at him only briefly to acknowledge appreciation for his service but hey, presto, his smirk is all gone. "But then, you're my key witness," Martin continues. "You must have seen me strike out at least twice."

"There were more?" I ask, as he obviously must be assuming that I witnessed more than I have.

"Online dating," he says, wearily. "I should ask for a refund."

I've no idea what online dating is all about except that to me, it looks just a step up from going on a series of blind dates, which sounds a little short of horrendous.

"Perhaps they were too young for you?" I suggest, remembering my conversation with Steve concerning the alleged vapid priorities of younger women.

"Yes," he agrees, as if I'm being very helpful. "I should definitely be with someone older; someone more mature."

"Why *do* you want to be with someone?" I ask him straight out. As soon as the question is out of my mouth, I feel surprised by my own bluntness; what a personal question to ask someone I just met, I chide myself. His reaction surprises me, however. Instead of telling me to mind my own business, he seems to be thinking deeply about the question.

"Actually," he says, pausing as if choosing his words with care. "I'm really trying to get a date to go with me to my ex-girlfriend's wedding. She sent me an invitation."

"And you're going to go?" I ask, wondering what kind of a woman sends an invite to a guy she just dumped; I'm assuming from the pained look on the poor guy's face that he was the one that got kicked to the curb.

"You don't think I should go?" he asks, his voice almost quivering with uncertainty. Wow, this has suddenly got strange. Someone's asking *me* for relationship advice? I can barely believe this young guy's honesty and the heartfelt way he has of being real and not seeming to want to hide his vulnerability like so many men... actually like *all* the men I've ever known. I don't think I've met one single man that didn't play games and seemed to want to defend against showing any display of vulnerability, as if their very lives depended on it. This young guys' innocence touches my heart.

"If you do go, you should show up with someone hot," I say, as if I'm feeling suddenly antagonistic towards this woman that I've never even met and making assumptions like she's sending him an invite for the sole purpose to rub his face in her new-found happiness.

It occurs to me that I could be completely wrong in my wild speculation, yet something inside me is being awoken by this young man; something that I didn't even know was dormant and perhaps has been sleeping for a very long time: my own sweetness and naiveté.

I used to be so sweet and naïve that I think the caption of my photograph in the high-school year book referred to me as the Naïve Queen of Sweetness or some such bullshit. I never had a problem with my so-called naivety but others seemed to think that I was either unintentionally hilarious, an easy touch for the manipulative or too just "soft" for my own good and was only setting myself up for constant hurt by being so "innocent:" as if innocence was considered some kind of defect or something.

Encouraged by others, as well as the hard knocks of life experience, to "harden" myself up, and wake up to reality, I think that I've just spent the last decade or so doing exactly that. So much so, that I've gradually become what some have described, both behind my back and sometimes to my face, as an angry bitch.

Seeing a part of myself in the tender eyes and sensitive heart of this young man, I'm suddenly feeling protective towards him and even though I don't know him from Adam, I don't want to see him get hurt.

"When is the wedding?" I ask him.

"Less than three weeks," he says as if he's feeling the scary pressure of a ticking clock.

"What's the actual date?" I ask, as if I'm considering being his date, which I totally am.

"The twelfth? Why?" he asks, his lower lip almost quivering with nervousness or maybe excitement, or both.

"I'll go with you," I tell him and I can see him restraining his inner teen that wants to yell and scream with joy.

"Seriously?" he asks, as if he's not sure he heard me right or maybe he thinks that he's being punked.

"Email me the details," I say as I take out a business card from my purse. It makes me feel so good to see a huge smile of relief break out on his face as his entire body relaxes.

CHAPTER 4

By the time we had finished our meal, John the waiter's killer smile had returned and he asked us very politely if we were ready for some coffee and desert, which Martin and I both decline. I get the impression that John the waiter doesn't take Martin too seriously as either a VIP customer of the restaurant or as a rival for my affections so, in the end, he doesn't seem too put out.

I had a really nice time chatting with Martin and when we leave the restaurant and he suggests that we check out the bar next door, I immediately accept. I have passed this bar so many times and always felt curious about what it was like inside... so here is my chance. One drink won't kill me and besides, it's still too early for my bed time. The thought of going home to an empty apartment has extremely low appeal.

The place is busy and buzzing with an energy that I quickly find exciting. I feel like I'm on the town on a school night and I very much like it. I can't remember the last time I was actually in a bar like this; young people talking excitedly and having fun; giant TVs mounted behind the bar showing mostly sports.

Like a proper gentleman, Martin opens the door for me and once inside, he lets me lead. I immediately spot two stools at the bar, which I made a bee line for. It's natural for me to gravitate to bar stools because that's where the TVs are and Bill always liked to watch whatever game was playing. The sport didn't seem to matter, except maybe tennis, which wasn't his favorite.

I never cared much for watching sports but I soon

discovered that if I wanted to spend more quality time with Bill, it was better for me to join him in his pursuits rather than insist that he give up some of his in order to meet me half way. Bill never really did like meeting me halfway in anything and when he did, I could tell that he resented it.

"Wow, the Lakers are losing to Dallas," I say looking up at the game on the TV. "Didn't see that coming," I say to Martin as he settles into his seat. "Two draft Buds," I automatically say to the busy bartender when he quickly scoops up some empty glasses from the previous occupants.

Realizing that I just ordered what Bill and I always order when we were in a similar situation, I turn to Martin, who has a wild grin of happiness on his face. "You drink beer, right?" I ask him.

"Oh, yeah," he says, looking as happy as a clam.

"What about sports? Are you into basketball?" I ask.

"Sports were the bane of my high school years," he answers, looking a bit pained. "Not the athletic type."

"Yeah, me neither," I concur.

"What is it with women and jocks?" he then asks and I hesitate to answer as I'm not sure of his question. "Everyone knows that jocks are assholes, right? I mean it's become something of a cliché, right?"

"Yeah," I answer tentatively, still not knowing where he's going with this.

"So why do all the pretty girls...?" he asks but then stops as if he's evaluating how he's coming across by even asking the question.

"Why do pretty girls like assholes?" I say, helping him out.

"Yeah," he says, smiling with relief and appreciation. "I mean they pretty it up by calling them bad boys but really... they're assholes. I don't get it."

"It's probably the same reason that men like bitches. I read a whole book about the subject but I still don't get it, either," I say.

Martin looks at me like he's just found someone that finally gets him and, in a way, I think I do. He's easy to talk to. As if he has so little defenses up, I feel like I don't have to put up any to counter him... and what a difference it is.

"Do you think that, in some way, people, deep down don't feel like they are worthy of love? Of being loved or something?" he asks and I visibly open my eyes wide in surprise at his insightful questioning.

"Wow," I say. "My therapist would love you."

"How else can you explain why someone would deliberately get involved with someone that they know to be... reprehensible?" he asks, pausing to carefully select his last word, which I admit is a bit strong.

"Okay," I tell him, moving closer so as not to be overheard. "I'm going to tell you a secret."

Moving in closer to me, he almost licks his lips in anticipation.

"Women are attracted to bad boys not because they want to fall in love..."

"Okay," he says, encouraging me to continue when I pause.

"Women are attracted to bad boys because of their looks; usually they're hot as all get out..." I say, pausing again.

"Okay," he says again with a hint of impatience.

"But mostly, they look at these hot, sexy bad boys and think... OMG this guy looks like he is killer in the sack."

Martin lets out a little grunt/snigger and smiles like he's just been inducted into the forbidden inner sanctum of the 'girl's only' secret society. His little boy glee is so cute; it encourages me to elaborate even further. "The things that this bad boy could do to me in bed... he could send me to the moon and back," I say with dramatic zest. "This guy could light up my world; he could touch me in places no decent guy can even imagine..."

"Seriously?" Martin asks.

"Seriously," I answer. "Think about it. If given the choice between a once-in-a-lifetime thrill ride and ... or let me put it this way... you go to Disneyland: do you want to play it safe and go for a spin in the tea cups or do you want to ride the bad boy thunder mountain roller coaster space rocket and scream your head off with fright and delight for the entire experience?"

"Okay," Martin says, his body sitting back upright. "When you put it like that..." he says, thinking it over. "That's a lot of pressure to be putting on bad boys," he considers. "Never thought I'd see the day when I almost feel sorry for them."

"Hey, don't. Nine times out of ten they never deliver on their promise. Most women that take the ride regret it and only wake up feeling icky the next day. No amount of showers can get rid of that amount of self-disgust."

"Okay," he says, looking at me with eyes that suggest that he knows I'm talking from experience.

"Yeah, I've taken the ride a few times," I admit. "So not worth it."

Martin smiles and takes a drink. I can tell that he's totally enjoying himself and as for me? I'm having a blast. We order more beers and talk about stuff that I don't usually get to talk about, which is so refreshing, I feel like I'm glowing. I haven't felt this much happy energy flowing through my body since I don't know when.

Boy, I just had a shocking realization: if this little bit

of excitement makes me so wonderfully happy... I must be a hugely depressed person the rest of the time. How friggin' sad is that?

"Okay, so I've a question," Martin says, almost giddy, now that he feels like he can get any secret girl question answered that he wants. "Why do women always want to change a guy?" he asks but then makes a face like he's not happy as if he thinks that he's asked the wrong question. Then he changes his expression, losing the unhappy face and makes a face that suggests that he was happy with his question all along. Is he drunk already?

"Why are women always unhappy with a guy? Like they want to turn them into someone that they would want and are not accepting of the someone that they actually are?" he asks.

"Well, first off, I don't know what kind of women you've been dating," I answer, thinking about the meaning of his questions. As I'm doing so, I quickly find myself in some kind of hall of crazy mirrors place in my mind that finds his question ridiculously funny. "But, let's face it. Most men are such assholes, they need changing in order to get them to function in meaningful society," I say, almost giggling.

Luckily, he doesn't take offence and instead, he giggles and stretches his hand up top for a high five, which I meet with such force that I almost hurt myself.

"Men are dumb-asses," I continue, encouraged when he sniggers even more. "If left to their own devices they'd just drink beer, play with themselves all day, eat crap food and play video games, until their eyelids closed shut from sheer exhaustion. If women didn't take an interest in them, they'd be total... irresponsible losers; incapable of holding down a job, cooking their own food or washing their own clothes..."

Martin is now laughing so hard, his beer is almost coming back up through his nostrils.

"Men should be thanking us for our care and compassion," I continue, on a roll. "We're the ones that have to put up with their shit while we support them through college and guide them into careers where they make shit-loads of money so they can download more porn. Meanwhile, we're in the background, ironing their shirts and getting their suits pressed; preening their nose hairs and making their hair and dental appointments... and what thanks do we get?"

"Stop it," Martin says feebly, laughing so hard, it looks like he's getting a muscle cramp just below his spleen.

"No thanks is the thanks we get," I say, with no intention of stopping. "We get you guys on the straight and narrow, help you make successes out of your lives and all the time we're being told to stop with the nagging..." I say, making myself laugh. "I'm sorry, Martin," I then say with mock seriousness. "What was your question?"

Martin is too teary-eyed with laughter to respond so instead he high-fives me again as if to say, 'Girl, you are a riot,' and surprising myself, I secretly agree: I never knew I could be this funny.

The evening degenerates into even more foolishness as if, for some reason, neither of us can have a serious conversation and once the giggles begin, they cannot be stopped. At one stage of our craziness, we even role-play, taking turns to "analyze" each other as if we are therapist-patient and we can determine each other's attitudes towards love and romance. I think that I've been so busy being serious all the time that I've forgotten what it's like to be frivolous. Now that I'm drinking from the well of ridiculousness once more, I'm finding it liberating and maybe even a little intoxicating.

After our night of beers and bullshit, we are both in no shape to drive home so we call a couple of cabs; one to take each of us to almost opposite parts of town; him to the valley and me to Santa Monica. He extends his hand to me so as to shake hands goodnight, which I find adorable and as he does so, I pull him to me and kiss him on the cheek, which, by his reaction, he clearly relishes. What a sweet and sensitive young man.

True to my word, the next morning I get up early and do an hour of yoga and a little bit of meditation. I have a hard time focusing because I can't stop smiling to myself and thinking fondly about the night before. I know that kids go to bars pretty much every night of the week but for me, the previous evening was what I would consider a wild and crazy night. I must be getting old.

I keep thinking of the things I was saying and all the goofing around... it was so much fun. *I* was so much fun! It's almost as if I have to ask myself: who was that person that came out to play last night? I mean, how many people do I know would describe me as a fun person? Not many and even those that would... I'd have to go back a long, long time.

I'm sure the booze played a part in my sudden return to revelry but then again, usually alcohol has the opposite effect; I usually become sad and morose and people want to sit away from me rather than towards me.

Maybe it's because Martin is such a disarmingly goofy guy that I feel safe enough to show my own goofy side. I can see his face looking at me now; he was so into me and even though the bar was crowded, it was as if no one else existed for him. He looked at my face all the while and I never once caught him looking over my shoulder to see if he could spot someone cuter that he might be missing. Can't say that for too many guys I know… or was married to, hint, hint.

I'm on so much of a high that I approach the stage project with gusto and enthusiasm. The ideal design obviously has to be something very abstract and I skim the stage directions again to see what characters are being directed to sit and if so, where and when. It would help for me to know the actor's on-stage movements and blocking but that won't happen until they begin rehearsals, which, mental note to myself, I should ask Ronald.

As if he read my mind, Ronald calls. "Hey, Ronald, I was just thinking of you," I answer.

"Only good thoughts, I hope," he says, sounding more upbeat than the last time we spoke. "How's the project going?"

"I meant to ask you when they start rehearsals. It would help to know the blocking."

"Don't worry about that. I talked to the director and they're entirely flexible. They're working on the assumption that there is no set, just open space."

"So, what are we doing designing a set?" I ask, more than a little mystified.

"The back drop will be important and we need to talk to the lighting guys because lights are playing a big part in their set changes… I know this is all so iffy so bear with me but it's almost like they want us to come up with ideas and sell them on what set they should go with."

"Great," I say, not really sounding great.

"On a completely different note… what are you doing this Friday night? I need you to come to a party with me."

"You're inviting me to a party?"

"It's for work and will probably be very boring. We need to make an appearance, that's all."

"Where's it at?"

"It's at the house of the guy we met that works for Paramount, Rich Tolliver?"

"Oh, yeah. Of course I'll come with you."

"Thank you so much, I'll owe you. Getting their business would be huge, a really big deal."

"Anything else?" I ask, anxious now to get off the phone.

"That's it. I'll fill you in on the details later in the week."

"Cool. See ya," I say, hanging up. I place my phone prominently on the table beside me so that I'd see it light up on an incoming call. I was expecting that Martin would be anxious to connect with me and we could both go over and laugh about the previous evening. I check to make sure that I keyed his phone number into my phone, which, I did.

Maybe I'll give him a special ring tone for when he calls and I'm thinking that something from the Beach boys would be appropriate. I go online and scroll through their tunes. The totally correct option jumps right out at me and I pay to download it: *Good Vibrations,* one of my all-time favorites.

CHAPTER 5

I wake up and straight away check my phone: no calls or texts. We're on day three now and still there is no call from Martin: did he lose my phone number?

Multiple thoughts swirl around my head: he didn't have as much fun as I thought he had; he's still serial dating and compiling a shortlist; I'm too old for him to even consider having as a friend; he's playing the wait-three-days and then call her phone game... I can hear Dr. Roberts in my head asking me how does that make me feel? Undesirable and unlovable, I answer right away.

I can't face morning yoga so I blow it off and I definitely can't stomach another torturous session of the stage project. I hate every single one of the twenty preliminary sketches that I've drawn up so far. As I sip my morning coffee, I look out through the front window and notice how beautiful the day is. It's time to get out of the apartment and take a stroll through the Third Street promenade; people watching and window shopping among the fashion stores always cheers me up.

As I walk into the huge bookstore at the top of the promenade, I head directly to the self-help section. It's been a while since I've been here but it feels like I'm returning home. I spent so much time here over the years, not to mention spending so much money buying almost entire shelves of books.

I think I've either read or recognize every relationship book on display. I've read all about the love languages; why men and women want different things from a relationship; why men marry bitches; why women worry too much and of course, all about the different planets that the two sexes originate from.

I'm sure a lot of what I've read helped but, realistically, I should have been reading these books *before* I got pregnant with Janice and not twenty years later when, for the third time in my life, the man I love decides to pack his bags and leave.

In fairness to Steve, I was the one doing the leaving but he said he was aware of the risks going in: getting involved with a young single parent who was feeling bereft and emotionally vulnerable. What does an eighteen year old know about relationships... or being pregnant, for that matter?

I pick out two books that I haven't seen before: one is about putting Zen into relationships and the other about hidden fears that couples don't know they have that can sabotage their intimacy. The blurb on the back of both books look good so I take them to the register. Grabbing a large tea from the coffee shop next door I decide to stroll over to one of my most favorite places in Santa Monica: the Palisades Park, which overlooks the ocean.

In the past, while sitting on one of the park benches looking out to sea, I've seen diving pelicans, dolphins, porpoises and of course, lots of surfers. The sunsets here are extraordinary; you can actually see the sun vanish beneath the ocean, as if it was knowingly dunking itself into the beautiful blue-green water.

I take out my purchases and skim through the Zen book first. I do a kind of Zen meditation in the mornings after my yoga, which is really simple and all about paying attention to the breath and to the body. It's very grounding, as well as relaxing and if I can discipline myself to do it regularly, it really helps me stay calm throughout the remainder of the day. I've have no idea how my limited ideas of Zen would apply to relationships so hopefully the book will explain in depth.

From what I gather from the table of contents and introduction, it requires that couples pay attention to their partners the same way that I pay attention to my body, I'm assuming. Of course, it seems to involve the one thing that most men I know seem to hate: talking about their feelings.

I put the book down in frustration and look out at the wide expanse of open blue sea. It pisses me off that it's only women that read these books. In all the years I've been in the relationship section of bookstores I've seen maybe a handful of men browsing the bookshelves and most of those were only there because their significant others were taking them there by the hand.

Why is it that only women seem to care enough about relationships to want to fix them? What's the point of me or any other woman reading relationship-improvement books if our partners are not as equally involved? It takes two people to play a game of tennis... hey, that should be a book title, right there!

Bill's response to my suggestions of self-improvement was the same answer he always gave about everything I encouraged him to do: 'Yeah, I don't know. Let's see how it goes,' he'd say, thinking that he sounded perfectly reasonable.

'Yeah... let's see how it goes...' pretty much summed up our entire marriage, come to think of it. A few times he'd say, 'let's just go with the flow,' until I told him that the only thing that goes with the flow is a dead fish and he promptly stopped using the term. It wasn't original on my part, I had read the dead fish phrase in a relationship book but it totally worked.

Not only did Bill and I *not* talk about our feelings, we barely talked about anything at all; anything that truly mattered, at least... like having kids, for instance. In the beginning, we both said that we wanted a family of our own. Janice was still just a baby but Bill treated her as his own and he always said that he'd love to have a boy... or a girl, he'd then say... let's see how it goes.

A few years had passed and even though we weren't using any birth control, no little babies, boys or girls, were coming along. Even though I suggested that we maybe get tested or explore if one of us might have a problem, his answer was still, 'no, let's wait and... see how it goes.'

"Doesn't it bother you?" I remember asking him. "Not to the point of getting the medical profession involved," he'd answer. "We don't need to be going crazy taking fertility drugs and all that crap... let's not go down that road," he said like going down that road was, what, the road to hell and damnation?

"Let's just get a few tests done, then," I suggested more than once.

"There's no panic," he'd answer. "Let's just see how it goes..."

Ugh... his laid back attitude used to drive me mad and when I kept persisting that we just might have a problem that could be easily fixed, he'd treat me like I was being irrational or unnecessarily creating a crisis that was putting a, 'strain on our marriage.'

As far as I was concerned, *not* talking about stuff was putting a strain on our marriage but he didn't like to see it that way. It's as if a problem didn't exist until we both mutually decided that we had a problem. However, the real problem was that he would never agree that we had a problem to begin with.

I didn't know how to successfully deal with that logic and as more time went by, we grew more and more apart. In his estimation we had a problem-free marriage. Even though I knew otherwise, I didn't know how to get him to see the truth or what language to use to get him to hear and understand me: it was like there was a glass wall between us and I had no idea how to reach him.

You can't fix the problem that you don't want to see and as I helplessly watched the impending train wreck of our marriage get closer and closer, I knew that someday all the unresolved problems were going to band together and jump up and bite him in his laissez-faire ass. Getting to say, 'I told you so,' ended up being no consolation... at all.

Feeling hungry, I decide that I should go home and put together some lunch, maybe some hot soup and a sandwich. I'll maybe then have a nice cup of coffee and attack the stage project again; Ronald needs to know that I'm making some progress, at least.

Just as I'm making my lunch, I've sliced into the thick bread and am placing veggies and cheese on it, Ronald calls. "Hey there," I answer cheerfully.

"Hey there," he says, matching my upbeat tone. "I have good news and bad news. Which do you want first?" he asks.

"Bad news first," I say.

"Bad news is I can't make the party on Friday," he says.

"That's fine with me," I say with relief, "I wasn't looking forward..."

"Hold that thought," he interrupts. "I wasn't finished with the bad news. I need you to go along, anyway."

"By myself?" I ask, not liking the idea one bit.

"You can invite anybody you want, obviously, and you really don't have to go, if you don't want... but it's such an important account and as you know, I've been working

on them for ages... just to make an appearance would be...
I'd so totally owe you."

"And you can't make it because?" I ask.

"That's the good news," he says and I can almost
hear him smiling. "Frank wants me to go up and meet his
sister."

I digest as best I can what Ronald is telling me but
all I can think about is what a self-obsessed jerk he is. "I'm
sorry, Ronald," I say, trying not to sound snarky, "but I'm
still waiting for the good news."

"This is huge," Ronald exclaims. "Frank wants me to
meet his family... well, his sister, not the parents, just yet
but don't you see how important that is? How this is like
such a... milestone? She's visiting him very briefly so if I'm
going to meet her, it has to be now... I thought you'd be
happy for me," he then says.

I'm too mad to say anything, so I don't.

"If you don't want to go to the party, then don't,"
he says. "I'll perfectly understand."

"I don't want to go to the party," I say.

"Not a problem," he says, sounding like it's a
problem.

"I'm really happy that Frank is taking your
relationship to the next level," I say and I know what I'm
saying sounds hollow and unconvincing.

"Thanks," he says, equally unconvincing. "I'll talk to
you later."

When he hangs up, I feel like shit. Even though I
think he's acting like a jackass, I still feel like I should have
been more supportive. Aside from the fact that he is more
or less my boss, I, of all people, should understand the
stupid lengths that we go to in an attempt to try and make
relationships work. At the same time, the thoughts of going
alone to a party, full of people that I don't know, does not

at all sound appealing, to say the least. Instead of coffee, I think it's time to open a fresh bottle of wine.

A few glasses of wine works wonders to my mood as I sketch away on the purgatory project and let my imagination and creativity run riot. I probably won't be able to use any of the hair-brained, scary-looking sketches I'm dreaming up but I'm having fun and the uninhibited wildness seems to be doing wonders for my creativity.

Just as I start a new sketch, my phone starts playing *Good Vibrations.* As if I can't help myself, I start singing along until I soon realize that I'm getting a call from Martin. A huge smile breaks out on my face and I suddenly feel like a bashful teenager as I joyfully take his call.

"Hello?" I answer, as if I don't know who is calling.

"It's Martin," he says and I surprise myself when I feel all gushy inside.

"Hello, Martin," I say as if I just turned into a sultry sex kitten. What is wrong with me? "I'm glad you called," I say. "I've been thinking a lot about you." I can almost hear his Adam's apple readjust itself in his throat as if he wasn't expecting to get sexy Frances this early in the evening.

"What have you been thinking?" he asks, matching my mood as if he wants to play, 'who's been a naughty girl today, then?' or some such role-playing sex game.

"Ooooooh," I purr, totally getting into character, "yummy thoughts."

"I've been thinking yummy thoughts about you, too," he says.

"What are you doing?" I ask him and even I am not sure what way I want him to answer.

"I'm on my way home from a job," he answers, beginning to sound more normal. "I looked at the beautiful sunset and thought of you."

"You are a romantic chappie," I say, now apparently

a sexy English lady. "I like it."

"What are *you* doing?" he then asks like it was a real question. "What do you do professionally?"

I realize that now he wants to have a normal conversation so it's actually good that he's saving me any further embarrassment as I don't seem to be able to stop myself. Had I received any further encouragement, I would probably have devolved into a naughty French maid that wanted to spank his cute little bottom or something. Somehow this guy brings out the madness in me and I may have to bring this up in therapy to find out exactly why.

When I tell him what my occupation is and what I'm working on, yada, yada, I can tell that my voice is beginning to sound more typical of how a mature responsible adult should sound. When he comes right out and asks me how old I am, I sober right up.

"Thirty-eight," I answer right back.

"Really?" he asks, like, what... he thinks I'm making it up? "Is that ancient?" I ask him back, assuming that that's how a guy in his twenties would describe my vintage. He then stutters nervously and gives me a compliment about how I look much younger for my age and 38 isn't old... yeah right.

I appreciate his efforts, though, and it's actually good to be having this conversation and to get it out of the way. If it's too much for him to handle he can move on and there's no harm done. Bearing that in mind I decide to pile it on and tell him that I've been divorced for three years; I've been married for fourteen years and my ex-husband is ten years older, which in twenty-speak would be way more than ancient, like, antique, even.

I wanted to get it all out there and tell him about Janice and Steve and runaway Jim Costas but he stops me before I could fully declare my hand because it seems it's too much information for him to handle so soon and he's getting totally freaked out. Just as I'm expecting him to tell me that it was nice meeting me, anyway, and gently hang up for good, he surprises me.

"I have an idea," he says. "We keep interviewing each other like this and we'll just freak each other out and never get past a first date. Let's just spend some time together. Whatever gets revealed, gets revealed. Deal?"

"Deal," I gladly agree and I can actually feel a wave of relief run from my head down to my toes. "Before you go," I say quickly, "want to come to a party Friday night?"

"Yeah, love to," he answers brightly.

When I put down the phone I feel like I just made everybody happy, myself included. I call Ronald and give him the good news and he thanks me hugely, like I just made his night. "I owe you big time," he says and when I put down the phone from his call, I give myself a major pat on the back. The world is back revolving on its axis the way it should. Maybe I'll put on some Beach Boys music.

CHAPTER 6

I surprise myself by waking up in dread and it takes me a few minutes of mental searching to understand why: today is Friday and in the evening I'm going on a date.

Waking up and feeling instant anxiety used to be my norm but I haven't woken up with this level of angst in quite some time. It makes me think that something is wrong and a behavior adjustment is necessary. As I throw on some clothes, I'm thinking of how best to cancel the whole thing and send the goofy young man packing.

I've no right to be dating someone so young; in fact, I shouldn't be dating anybody; I should just forget the whole man thing and... oh, I don't know what to think; I just hate feeling like I've got a swarm of spiders in my chest trying to crawl and scrape their way out of me.

I swore I'd never take another pill but I'm sorely tempted to swing by Dr. Roberts and pick up a prescription from her. I change my mind when I think back to all the days, weeks and months that I spent in a mental haze and an emotional numbness. At best, I was maybe existing but I certainly wasn't living; I barely have a memory of anything during those years and yet those years passed me right by, as if I wasn't even there. The clock was ticking but nobody was home. I got older and had nothing to show for it.

I did promise Ronald that I'd show up, though, so to cancel would really mess things up between us. I guess I just have to grit my teeth and make it through the day and night, see it through. When I look in the bathroom mirror I almost frighten myself: I look like crap. My eyes are puffy, my skin looks blotchy and my hair looks dry and lifeless.

Getting old is not for the faint of heart, that's for sure.

I sit down at the kitchen table and grab a notepad: I need to plan my day. I know myself well enough at this point to realize that if I have any gaps in the day, when I have nothing to do, I'll only spend that time in useless worry. I'll then tell myself that it's okay to open a bottle of wine and a few glasses later I'll be blowing everyone off and disconnecting my phone. It's a slippery slope.

If I manage to fill up the day with back-to-back activity, then the evening will come soon enough and I know then that I'll make it through. So first thing I write down is 'one hour yoga,' followed by 'Zen meditation,' like, twenty minutes. Also, I should call Ronald and get him to swing by on his way to the airport so I can hand off these sketches. I need his feedback and I don't want to wait any longer not knowing if I'm on the right track or not. Based on his feedback, let's say I work at that for two hours.

I should go get my hair done and maybe meet someone for lunch: this is all perfectly doable. Steve is always available to do lunch: 'call Steve,' I write down. My backup should be Janice... actually not Janice because we've just been ending up in shouting matches our last few meetings. If Steve can't make it, I'll see if my friend Karen is free for a few hours. I can do this.

Steve and Stacy greet me on the patio of the trendy Westside eatery and we sit at a table shielded from the sun by a huge umbrella. Although I've heard her name mentioned, this is the first time I'm meeting Stacy and from my first impression: she looks very young. Steve runs his own art gallery and he does quite well, or so he says. With her tattoos and funky, bohemian outfit, Stacy does not look like the type of person who runs in the same social circles.

"Where did you guys meet?" I ask.

"Stacy's a masseuse," Steve answers by way of explanation.

"You get massages?" I ask Steve, surprised that he never mentioned getting one.

"I do now," he says, nudging his smiling date as if they have a secret they don't feel like sharing.

"We were introduced by mutual friends," Stacy tells me, which is really not telling me, which is fine. Steve seems to have a new girlfriend every other month and I probably don't want to know where he really picks them up.

"What do you feel like eating today, ladies?" Steve asks, opening the menu like he has an appetite. "My treat."

It feels weird having lunch with them both and not really having anything in common to talk about. I'm more used to Steve being on his own where he seems more real as a person and acts less like he's putting on a performance, which he tends to do when others are around. It's probably because I've seen him at his most private and vulnerable that perhaps he allows himself to be less guarded when we're alone together.

"You guys go way back, huh?" Stacy asks, looking at me.

I've no idea what Steve has told her of our history so I'm not sure how to answer. "We sure do," I say, taking a page from their play book.

"That was such a long time ago, huh, Frances?" Steve says. "You were like... eighteen or something?"

"Yup," I agree.

"And you had a child?" adds Stacy. "That must have been rough."

"She turned out to be a lovely young lady," I say, still giving nothing away. When I do think back to whom I was back then, it's as if I was a completely different person. I was madly in love with Jim Costas, my college boyfriend and it was hugely shocking for me to have him dump me when I told him that I was pregnant with his child.

The fact that I had little home support only made a bad situation worse. My mother had very little sympathy for me and seemed to be taking the position of, 'see, this is what you get when you... fill in the blank.' The fact that her husband – my father – abandoned us all years earlier probably played into her attitude but she was no help to me and my predicament.

I've been over this so much in therapy and I certainly don't want to be sharing it now but when Steve came along, it was like he was my knight in shining armor. Even though he knew I didn't love him like I loved Jim, he told me that that was okay and that our love would grow to be something different; that he would take care of me and that everything was going to be okay. At the time and in the troubled state I was in, that was music to my ears.

"You sound like you're very proud of her," Stacy says and I nod in agreement as I drink some water. "How old is she now?" she then asks.

"She just turned twenty," I answer and I can see her react with some thinly disguised shock. "Did you think she'd be younger?" I ask.

"I guess," she says. "She's almost the same age I am."

I don't ask Stacy's age and I don't need to but I can see her thinking that she's dating someone old enough to be her father; or maybe she's not, perhaps it's just my own biased speculation.

"Whatever happened to that young guy that was crushing on you?" Steve asks me. "In the restaurant?"

"We went for a drink," I answer. "I had a very nice time. He's a very nice... young man," I say and when I hear myself talking like this I wonder what in heaven's name am I doing?

Sitting across from Steve and the much younger woman that is his date makes me realize how crazy I'm being. Do Martin and I look just as... idiotic, sitting with each other as a couple out on a date? Do people look at us and wonder if we are a mother and her son having a drink to celebrate his college graduation or something?

"Of course it's much more socially acceptable for the man to be older; what a double standard, huh?" Stacy says, presumably trying to make me feel better.

"It still doesn't make it any less pathetic," I instantly think but I surprise myself when I hear myself saying it out loud... oops. "I mean..." I instantly begin to say when I see both sets of their eyes open wide with surprise, "... society having such a double standard and openly discriminating against women is... pathetic," I conclude, hoping to redeem myself.

"I'm not complaining," Steve says with a goofy-looking smile and I have to restrain myself from slapping him or throwing a glass of water into his smug face; even if he is trying to be funny.

"Are you seeing him again?" Stacy asks with a tone that is soft and compassionate.

"I think he could be a good friend," I answer. "We seem to get along well together."

"The main thing is that you can be friends with who you're with, right?" says Steve as if he's saying it for Stacy's benefit. I feel like challenging him and asking him that if that's the case, why does he insist that every date he goes out with be a... what does he call it: a "looker?" Talk about your double standards...

"For most of history women didn't have a say about who'd they be married to so I would imagine if you didn't at least become friends with your spouse... you were in for a very long and lonely term of imprisonment," Stacy says and surprises me that she could say something so thoughtful.

"That's very well said," I agree. "We take it for granted now that women can choose to marry the man they 'fall in love with.' But the idea of romance is a very modern one, well said."

"Sometime late in the middle ages," Stacy adds and we both share a sisterly moment by clinking our glasses together. "To romance," she toasts.

"To happiness," I say instead because nobody at this table wants to hear what I have to say about the high-jacking of romance by our modern, capitalist-consumerist society.

"Oh, before I forget," says Steve. "Your mom invited us to her birthday party, so we'll both see you there."

"You're still in touch with my mom?" I ask, knowing that, of all the men in my life, Steve was always her favorite. Maybe because he picked up the slack where she fell down, I'm not surprised that she'd feel maybe some way indebted to him.

"We send each other birthday cards every year, that kind of thing. This one is a biggie for her, though. She's turning seventy?"

"Yeah," I agree.

"That's still young," Stacy chimes in. "Being seventy isn't like it used to be. We're all in better shape as we age than before, right?"

"I hope so," says Steve, smiling. "For your sake," he then says, tickling his date. It's time for me to leave, I think.

After lunch I get my hair done and I get back to the apartment just in time to meet with Ronald. "What do you think?" I ask him as he takes a look at my sketches.

"These are great," he says, surprising me. "There's

enough variety here to give them options. I think you did a great job."

"Thanks," I say gratefully.

"Of course it's early days, they may want to go in an entirely different direction, so we'll see," he says, his mind seeming to be elsewhere.

"Are you nervous?" I ask. "About meeting his sister? That's pretty big."

"Yeah. I didn't expect to be but his family is so old school. His sister's the only one that sounds any way... progressive," he admits. "Should I get her a gift or something? What do you think?" he asks nervously.

"You want to buy her affection?" I say with a smile.

"Sure. Why not?" he says, only half joking.

"Naw, I say. It's probably best if you don't try too hard. She's going to like you for you."

"You're sweet," Ronald says, putting away the sketches in his suitcase. "Maybe you can send me the digital copies also?" he asks.

"Of course. Have a really good time."

"I will," he says, giving me a departing hug. "Thanks again for going to the party. It means a lot. Hope you're taking someone fun."

"Me too," I say. "Me too."

I end up not doing any work on the stage project because Ronald didn't give me any useful feedback that I could work with, after all. That leaves me with three hours and sixteen minutes before I pick up Martin who, very conveniently, lives between me and Pasadena, which is where the party is. I don't know what I was thinking earlier in terms of time management but when I mentally compute travel time along with getting-ready time, I need every one of those minutes. The burning question in my mind, of course, is:

what am I going to wear?

Looking into my closet, which needs major reorganization, I look from my dresses to my jeans to my separates and I'm instantly panicked. First of all, the party is kind of business; at least, as well as looking smart and put-together, I also need to look like a creative, which in LA is a tricky combo.

This is also a date, my first date in... forever. What do people wear on dates, these days? Something hot and sexy? I can't look too trashy, obviously, but I also don't want to look like an office clerk or a school marm or something. I might be able to get away with a nice pair of jeans but then what if everyone else is going more formal? I'm pretty sure that if Ronald was going, he'd show up in his customary sports jacket and slacks. If I was going with him, I'd choose my outfit to match.

What would Martin be wearing? Should I call him or would that make him feel weird? I doubt if any of his dates have ever called him and asked him what he was wearing to the restaurant or to the bar that evening. He'd probably think that that's more like a question his mum would ask. Note to self: stop thinking about the age thing like it's a thing.

I decide to leave the clothes dilemma till later, after I bathe and do my makeup. While running a hot bath, I put on a face pack, light some candles and put on some soft music. Soaking in the bath calms me down and I love the scent of lavender from the bath bombs that Ronald gifted me with last Christmas. I spend so much time in the bath and in the bathroom in general, that when I check the time again I panic. When I mentally compute the remaining minutes to what should be my leave time I realize that I have a mere twenty minutes left.

When I was married, I was always the one that was

late or the one that was doing the last minute scrambling. I got used to Bill standing by the door with his keys in his hand, staring daggers at me as I ran around the house gathering up what we needed, some gifts to bring along to a party, maybe or frequently deciding at the last minute that I needed to change my outfit.

It used to bug me like crazy when he'd repeatedly say, "Are you ready now?" or "We need to go," over and over again and I'd tell him that he wasn't helping and that I'd be ready when I'm ready. As much as his impatience annoyed me then, I kind of miss it now. I miss him standing by the door, shuffling his feet and looking very, very annoyed. It's bizarre. The thing that used to feel awful at the time, I'm now looking back at with fondness.

Looking into my closet with greater urgency, I decide to default to what I know I look really good in: the skinny-fit tube skirt and matching top that I grabbed at Nordstrom's in their January sales. It's chic, hip and sexy and I always get the best compliments. Please lord I hope Martin doesn't show up in torn jeans and a t-shirt with the name of a heavy metal band emblazoned all over it. I should have called him.

Martin is waiting for me outside his apartment which I find a bit strange: does he have a wife or a live-in girlfriend or something? Is he ashamed of the state of his bachelor pad and he doesn't want me to see his living conditions?

Brushing aside my concerns, I get out of the car to give him a hug. He seems so happy to receive it that he holds me longer than a polite greeting, which I like. He's dressed very smartly and he actually looks really good. As we break from the embrace and share a smile, all my earlier anxieties vanish and I'm feeling glad I'm doing this, after all. He has such a kind face and his smile is so sweet and earnest, I feel like I could trust this man with my heart.

"You look amazing," he says as we get into the car and strap ourselves in. I smile like I'm a high-schooler and my face feels hot like I'm blushing.

"Thank you," I say. "You don't look too bad, yourself."

"Nice music," he says, noticing that my satellite radio music was still playing, which I had forgotten about.

"Thanks," I say, unsure about how to follow it up.

"You like music?" he asks, after a pregnant pause.

"I love music," I answer. "Play it all of the time... really helps with my mood."

"What music do you like?"

"I've an eclectic taste and it depends on my mood but I've been listening to a lot of angry chick music lately."

"What's angry chick music?" he asks and I smile because it's just something I made up.

"I don't think it's a genre but if there's a female singer sounding forceful and in her power singing about heartbreak and stuff... I'm all over it."

"Cool," Martin says and I can tell that he can't relate.

"I go through phases. I'm sure it's the same with you? What are you listening to?"

"I really don't listen too much. I mean, I do like music... it's just since high school when there was so much pressure to be listening to cool bands... I found myself telling people that I was into music that I wasn't... just so as not to sound like a dork, I guess."

"Yeah, all that peer pressure, right?" I say and I squirm as I'm saying it because I'm sure I'm sounding like some adult that read about high school peer pressure in the newspaper and want to let the younger kids know that I'm cool and that I understand. I wish he wouldn't keep mentioning high school, though. Every time he says it, it's like I switch into adult speak like high school was so long ago for me that it was another lifetime altogether.

"I don't like heavy metal," he then says, after another awkward pause.

"Me neither," I agree and I think I said it way too forcefully, like I've had a really bad experience with it in the past or something.

"I'm not crazy about hip-hop or rap," he then says and I'm now hoping that we're done with the music conversation. "Some jazz is okay," he then adds. "I don't like the freestyle stuff, though. When they improvise?"

"Yeah," I say, trying to think of something else to talk about.

"I like what you're playing, though," he says. "That's really nice."

"Thanks," I say. "I like to play this station when I'm driving."

"It's good driving music," he agrees.

"Yeah," I say and as I try to concentrate on driving and thinking of something more interesting to talk about, there ensues a long silence. Our previous night out together was so much fun, the conversation so spontaneous and witty, I'm wondering now if I was actually imagining that we were having a great time. Maybe because it was so long since I had been in a bar with a strange man that the occasion overwhelmed me and just like when you're cooped up in the house for so long and then you go out, it feels extraordinary; is that the same principle at work here? If this is how it's going to be for the rest of the evening, it's going to be a long night.

Perhaps the alcohol played a large part in our presumed togetherness; it wouldn't be the first time. As we all know, booze is renowned for lowering our inhibitions and allowing the inner madness to come out. As I pull onto the 134 freeway and merge with the speeding traffic, I'm thinking that if this whole date thing is a bust, it's going to be a huge relief. Maybe Martin will meet someone that he's crazy about, maybe a college student or something, and I can return to my normal life of... whatever. I don't really want to think of what my life is, right now.

Then again, what if he does meet someone more to his age and liking? How embarrassing would that be? Even if we're not the perfect match, you don't want to go to a party with a date and leave by yourself, looking like a loser. He doesn't have a car, so I'd probably be driving him and his date back to his place so they can get cozy and intimate. As I'm pulling away, I could tell him to have a nice evening and remind him to use a condom or something equally helpful.

When I hear my inner dialogue, sometimes I'm wondering who's doing the talking. Lately I'm beginning to sound like my mother or someone equally old and judgmental, which is distressing. I didn't think I had an age thing going on but now all I seem to be thinking about is age. It was easier with Bill because he was the older one and I was the trophy wife; until he replaced me with a younger trophy wife... why didn't I see that coming?

I was ten years younger than him but I didn't think about age with Bill and as far as I know, he didn't think about it either. Then again, if Bill was attracted to a younger woman, most likely he was thinking about it without ever saying anything. After the first few years of marriage, we hardly had sex at all and the occasions of our love-making just dwindled down to nothing. Of course he didn't want to talk about it; any time I brought it up, he'd give some excuse like being tired, stressed or some variation of "too much on his mind" nonsense-sounding bullshit.

He didn't consider that we had a problem, at least

not a problem to be concerned about because "all marriages go through a low period" or I think he called what we were going through a "blue patch" a few times. How effed up is it for someone to be thinking that their wife - the one that they are supposedly crazy about - is losing their looks to age and doesn't say a darn thing about it? He must have been thinking it; he barely touched me for most of the remaining years that we were married. I really don't know why he stopped wanting me or why it all went to shit… it just did.

I remember telling him that we had become more like roommates than a married couple and that it was a concern for me. Come to think of it, I gave him ample opportunity to voice his concerns, which he never did; except to say that I was nagging him or going on about things that didn't matter.

Maybe it had nothing to do with me and it was something that was going on with him. I read a lot about men and the middle-age, midlife crisis that a lot of them seem to be prone to. If women worry about crow's feet, turkey necks and saggy breasts, men worry about their virility and their loss of "youthful exuberance" as one book explained it.

If it's one thing that stuck in my craw the whole time I was married was that I had to try and decode what was going on in my husband's head the whole time. The two questions, "What is he thinking, what is he feeling?" was my version of a bad song that gets stuck in the head that, whether you like it or not, you just keep repeating and you can't seem to shake.

Dr. Roberts has a rock on her desk that's carved with the words, "Know thyself." The rock has been there forever and I think she said that it comes from an ancient Greek philosopher: the saying, not the rock. It's hard enough trying to figure myself out but why do I have to try and figure out someone else, someone who doesn't even seem that bothered about knowing themselves to begin with?

Is that really the option here: be alone and stay in my comfort zone versus be in a relationship and get challenged with stuff I don't particularly care to be challenged with? Dr. Roberts would call that growth, of course, because to her, everything that challenges us is a growth opportunity. I just don't know where the hell we're all supposed to be growing to or for what purpose. Can't I just be happy without the discomfort?

Do I get brownie points for putting myself out there tonight? Going to someone else's party hosted by people I don't really know and taking along a strange man that doesn't like to talk? Jeez, he's just staring out the window and pretending to like the friggin' music: isn't he going to say anything? "What are you thinking?" I finally ask him. "You seem like you're miles away."

"I was wondering what this party is going to be like," he answers and by the tone in his voice he sounds nervous, which would account for his silence, I guess.

I mustn't judge, I mustn't judge...

The poor guy is probably terrified out of his mind going to a strange party with a strange woman that's not talking to him so as to make him feel more accepted and needed. If it's one thing I've learnt from reading relationship books, it's that men need to feel needed and wanted. He was probably thinking exactly the same thing that I've been thinking about him and dreading going to this party just as much, if not more, than I am.

I should share my thoughts more and make him feel wanted.

"To be honest," I say, hesitating a bit, "I'm kinda

apprehensive about bringing you."

"How come?" he asks.

When I tell him that I've been conjuring up nightmare scenarios in my mind about him running off with some young sexy thing at the party, a smile breaks out on his face and a healthy rose color returns to his cheeks: I hadn't noticed how pale he had looked until his blood flow returns to his face. "I guess I'm afraid that someone young and really cute is going to make a play for you," I say with a warm smile.

Beaming a huge smile, Martin sits more erect in his seat, and whether he's conscious of it or not, his body leans closer in towards mine. "Forget it, Frances," he says, as if he's now the lead character in a Bogart movie, "not going to happen."

His smile and demeanor makes me smile and it's as if both our bodies relax at the same time. When he places his hand on mine, it makes me feel desirable and reassured: I'm now actually looking forward to the evening.

It's funny how we were both silent because we were both nervous and in our silence I was projecting all kinds of things onto him and second-guessing what he was thinking and feeling. I'm reminded of the Zen relationship book that I just bought and maybe this is what that's all about: being honest in communication at all times. I need to read more of that book...

CHAPTER 7

When we finally get to the party, I look around for who I might know. I see a few familiar faces of people I've worked with in the past but I don't know their names nor do I know them well enough to be having a meaningful conversation with. I do say hello to Rich and Eric, who are the key people that Ronald wants to impress, but they seem so concerned that everyone is having a good time that they aren't very chatty.

They do have their work cut out for them, however, as no one present seems to be having a good time. It's pretty typical of these kinds of occasions, I think, where people show up more from a sense of obligation rather than of genuine enthusiasm.

It's also the classic networking party where people are more concerned with making business connections than they are of having a good time. If you look closely enough, you'll see people meeting people for the express purpose of finding out what it is that the other person does, professionally. If their profession or their social standing can help out that person's career in any way, there will be a brief chat followed by the mutual exchanging of business cards. Then it's on to the next possible connection.

Pretty, pretty boring.

I smile at Martin who is watching and following me around like a cute little puppy dog. I take his hand and give him a big smile which I hope makes him feel more at ease. I feel now like he was the right choice and I'm glad I invited him. Not knowing anyone at this shindig makes me feel closer to him, maybe like it's us versus the anonymous crowd.

"Something to drink?" I suggest.

"Yes, please," he says, like a man in a desert parched for water.

They have a bartender guy serving at a makeshift bar and we both get a glass of red wine. Martin looks very much like he's out of his comfort zone and is probably worried about messing up in some socially inappropriate way. It makes me feel more protective of him and I smile to myself because, been there, done that, I know what he must be feeling.

I've felt so awkward in many a social situation before, especially when Bill would take me on one of his business functions or worse still, when we had to entertain clients at our house, which was totally nerve wracking, to be sure.

"So, tell me about yourself," I say to him as we get comfortable on a large sofa. "I know absolutely nothing about you. What do you do?"

As Martin gets comfortable on the sofa and tells me that he's a freelance photographer and goes on to explain how photography is his passion and why he loves it so much... I begin to get a fuller and more detailed picture of him beyond some "younger man" prejudices that I had been harboring in my mind all this time.

As the conversation transitions from one subject to the next, it's not so much his thoughts about current affairs or movies or LA traffic that interests me so much as how he is revealing to me his personality and the soul who lives inside the body of a man that was born some years later than me.

As he speaks eloquently about every subject that comes up – the usual conversational topics that Angelinos talk about – I can see how he has actually put some thought into his insights and isn't merely stealing his convictions from the news reports or prevailing consensus opinion. He strikes me more as an independent thinker than someone who accepts whatever the socially accepted attitudes are that define the current norms of thinking.

As we talk and talk, I forget about our age difference; I don't even think about it. It's not even remotely relevant. I also don't even think about Bill, which is actually really huge; when do I ever not think about Bill? I don't miss him nor did I compare him with Martin.

Martin seems to me to be one of a kind; I don't think I've met anyone quite like him. He's smart and funny but I can also see that he's very sensitive and thoughtful. I don't know many sensitive men; at least not the kind of sensitive man that isn't afraid of showing it.

I do believe that men are sensitive creatures, some perhaps even more so than many women perhaps but I also believe that they hide their vulnerabilities so deep that even they can't access their feelings anymore; or maybe they protect themselves with such macho posturing that they're not even aware that they're coming across like an unfeeling robot.

Martin gives me the respect and reverence of giving me his full attention when he talks and above all else... he listens. Maybe it's my many years in therapy that has shaped how I think and how I behave but I've come to realize that conversation has more to do with listening than with actually talking. That was a huge one for me to learn about and when I really understood it, it was like a light went on in my brain and I've looked at social communication differently ever since.

Let's face it, it's easy to talk and I think most people love talking about themselves and their opinions but do we really listen? Do we truly listen to what the other person is saying? For the longest time, I didn't. Well, I listened up to the point that the other person stopped talking and then I would tell them what I thought but really, I wasn't listening; I was just waiting for them to finish whatever point they were making so I could give them my two cents; which is the same two cents I always share on the subject... because my opinions rarely changed: it was always the same two cents.

I've since learned that that's not real communication. If I spout my ideas about something to someone else that then spouts their ideas about the subject back, then, what's the point? No one has really listened enough and subsequently hasn't thought deeply enough about what the other person is saying. Neither party is deeply affected by the other person's thoughts or even open-minded enough to thoughtfully consider the ideas shared and possibly change their minds.

For instance, whenever I'm caught in a situation where I'm listening to a Democrat talk to a Republican, I never say a word. I've been in enough of these political conversations to know that nobody is going to change anybody else's mind, no matter how articulate or passionate they are about what they're saying. I'm sure it may happen on rare occasions but I've yet to witness it.

I've no idea what political party Martin supports and I'm not going to ask. It's actually a no-brainer in Los Angeles because everybody is a liberal, at least in the circles I move about in and besides, in LA, politics isn't the major topic of conversation, movies are. I know that the rest of the country thinks that we're shallow, especially as the number two topic of conversation in La La land is traffic but, at the end of the day, if no one is truly listening to anybody else, we're all just making noise.

On the topic of movies, Martin surprises me by

telling me that his favorite genre is Romantic Comedy. He looks so cute when he says it, too: leaning in closer as if he's confiding a deep and dark secret; looking around in case he might be overheard. Being a sensitive guy must be tough. It must be tough because there seem to be so few of them, at least as far as I can tell. I think guys are hard on other guys and maybe all their softness is bashed out of them from a very young age. If they make it through high school with their gentleness intact, they should maybe be given a medal or something.

Once we get talking about romantic movies and romance, in general, I can barely contain myself. "Romantic love is what we're conditioned to believe *is* real love," I tell him and I'm encouraged because he really seems to be listening to what I'm saying. He thinks about what I'm saying, as if his mind is flexible and he could change his opinion if presented with a good argument.

"To define relationship solely in romantic terms is like describing marriage only by what a couple does on their honeymoon," I continue and I can see his eyes light up as if a light bulb went on in his head.

I'm loving our conversation.

When we were kids, Doris and I used to pay make-believe games. Although she was a couple of years younger, I'm pretty sure she was the one that decided what game to play most of the time. One of our favorites was, 'the wedding day.' Borrowing costumes from mom's closet, we took turns marrying each other off; it was magical. With mom's scarves, we'd make a veil for ourselves and clip together enough skirts and slips to make a long flowing bridal gown.

The fantasy of the wedding day has remained huge in my mind ever since, almost as if the aspiration of my life was to achieve the perfect wedding. I didn't have aspirations to become a scientist or an astronaut or the first female president or even to become an artist or an accountant: it was to have a perfect marriage.

I didn't know exactly what the details were, or even if any details were required or necessary, but the promise of happily ever after seemed to be filled with wide-ranging assurances all of its own; all-encompassing pledges that would seemingly ensure happiness to the end of my days.

It's easy to scoff now at such childish notions and consider them naïve and ridiculous even but there's very little spoken of in our culture to suggest otherwise. Happily-ever-after is still being peddled as the end game of all female pursuits and the only true indicator, hope and promise, of real and lasting happiness that we women will secure for ourselves in our lifetimes.

The happily-ever-after suggests great things: love, protection and security from a perfect mate, a beautiful house that could be a showcase for Architectural Digest as well as providing a perfect space to bring up happy and healthy children, the boys growing up to become astronauts and scientists.

The glue that holds the entire enterprise together is romantic love.

Without romantic love, none of this is possible and as long as romantic love remains, the sun comes up and the earth revolves on its axis, just the way that it should. When romantic love ceases to exist between the couple, the house of cards come crashing down; the home gets sold, the kids get to stay with a mum who must now must find a job – not a career, too late for that – and the dad goes off to see if he can find romantic love with someone else and maybe start all over again (if he didn't already find a better happily ever after with a younger woman, that is).

Of course, this only happens if we buy into the fairy

tale that is being peddled by Hollywood and the book, magazine, cosmetics and advertizing industries. If we had listened to our elders when they told us that marriage is not for the faint of heart; that marriage requires work and patience and character building and a willingness to change, to be flexible and non-judgmental, etc., etc., then maybe we would all have had a better chance at achieving true and lasting happiness, after all.

When I share all of this with Martin, I try not to sound bitter or angry but I also don't put a check on my passion. I put it all out there... and he loves it. For a single guy, who seems to have limited relationship experience, he seems to be totally on board with the whole, 'romantic love as the be-all and end-all is a crock' theory and, even though, like me, he loves the idea of romance, he doesn't seem fooled into thinking that that is the only thing to look for in a relationship.

I'm sure guys have their own myths and misconceptions to consider but I'm pretty sure that their idea of romance is not the same as the female version. I've yet to meet a man that even mentions the wedding day as being part of the overall romance package and from what I can gather from my female friends, sometimes it takes all they've got to get their guys passionate enough to even want to walk down that aisle of here-comes-the-bride with any level of enthusiasm.

Martin's eyes sear into me like I'm the most interesting person he has ever met, which I must admit is a turn on. He hasn't lifted his eyes from mine the whole time and seems unconcerned that there may be hotter-looking women strolling around the party displaying varying degrees of exposed boobs and flesh. When I do look around, I realize that we are only a few of the remaining people still at the party.

Typical for a networking party in LA, people do tend to leave early. I've heard someone explain the reason as being that either they have to arrive very early for work on a studio set the next day or they don't have a job but they leave early wanting to give the impression that they need to be working on a set first thing the next morning. Even though most creatives in LA do not consistently get work, there is a significant stigma attached to being unemployed.

"We should go," I say, even though I truly did have a terrific time. I say my goodbyes to the hosts and Martin and I stroll out into the lovely balmy evening. As we walk to the car, I can smell the beautiful scent of lilac from a nearby garden. Crickets are chirping loudly which adds to the beauty of our meandering stroll. I take his hand which he holds and then wraps around my waist, pulling me gently to him as we arrive at the parked car.

"Did you have fun?" I ask, expecting only a positive response.

"I'm having a blast," he says and even as I pause, holding his look long enough for him to register that I want him to kiss me, he hesitates... and the moment is lost. Although a minor one, it's our first misstep of the evening and as I let him into the passenger side door, I'm left wondering if he didn't kiss me because he misread the signal or because he choose not to.

As I pull out and head towards home, our conversation starts up effortlessly again and we take up exactly where we left off; still talking about movies and romance as if it was the most pressing puzzle to be solved with the survival of humanity itself at stake. I know that I can take myself so very seriously most of the time but talking with passion like this with Martin is a whole lot of fun. I'm more used to talking passionately with my female friends about equally trivial stuff so it's rare for me to have a guy be so similarly engaged.

Even if romance is not in our future I can tell straight off that Martin and I could truly be very good friends. That's something I've never had with a guy before. I don't think that I've felt this calm being with another man before, almost as if being with him takes all my anxiety away and I feel safe. I've only had one small glass of wine so I know that alcohol doesn't fully account for my feelings of peace and calm. Right now, I'm not worried about anything, almost as if everything is as it should be; things may not be perfect but all is well, nevertheless.

Maybe people give off different energy the same way that places and cities seem to. Any time I visit New York, for instance, I feel this buzz all the time, like I have to be doing something or going out somewhere, as if the city doesn't want me to sleep. Similar to the effects of caffeine, perhaps, New York is fun for me to visit but to stay there too long would probably burn me out over time.

Martin's effect on me is the opposite. With Martin I feel like I'm sitting on a bench in Palisades Park that overlooks the ocean and I'm feeling perfectly calm as I take in a beautiful sunset or maybe I'm sitting down on the beach just a few feet from the soft-sounding, gentle waves of the ocean. Even the sound of his voice makes me feel calm; it's so non-threatening and... soft, for want of a better description.

Getting back to my apartment seemed like it took no time at all. Apart from the fact that there was little traffic, our engaging conversation made time appear to go by very quickly. As I pour two generous glasses of red wine, Martin is sharing his opinion about romance and movies. "In the movies, they edit out the boring parts and..."

As he talks, and I pass him his glass of wine, I'm suddenly struck by the notion that I automatically drove home and didn't drop Martin off at his apartment on the way. In fact, I didn't even ask him if he wanted to go back to my place or anybody's place, for that matter; I simply drove home. Am I going to drive him back to his place or should I suggest that he crash on the sofa or something?

A wave of panic courses up through my body and I don't know what to do. What does he think of me inviting him in for a glass of wine? Is he expecting to have sex? Is he thinking that I'm expecting that we'll have sex?

Martin looks at me expectantly and I realize that he's stopped talking. "Exactly," I say, as if I was listening and agreeing to his every word. Realizing that I wasn't really listening to him, he seems to get a bit nervous and now, for the first time of our wonderful evening together, both of us are feeling strange with each other. I wish I knew what he is thinking or what his expectations are.

"I guess we solved the whole romantic love enigma," he says awkwardly.

"I guess we did," I say, just as awkwardly. "What are you in the mood for?" I then ask him.

"You mean like coffee versus wine or something?" he asks, shifting nervously in his seat.

Taking command of my nervousness, I place my wine on the coffee table and sit closer to him. I want that feeling of closeness that we had developed to return; I don't want us to be feeling weird with each other. Perhaps if we kiss for a bit, we might both loosen up and get reconnected; maybe even reconnect in a deeper way.

He continues to look at me strangely, which isn't helping, as if he's not quite sure what to do next. As he finally leans in to kiss me, his lower lip trembles like it's having an epileptic fit or something; it's not attractive.

When our lips touch... I don't feel anything very much, except weirdness. It's been so long since I kissed anybody so maybe I've lost my touch. Maybe the nerves and sensors in my lips that involve kissing have withered and died for lack of use, I don't know, but this feels... weird.

Martin seems to be enjoying it, however and I can feel him getting turned on as he gets more amorous. He doesn't seem to notice that I'm uncomfortable and I really want to go slower than the excitable pace he's setting for us both. His body feels hungry as he kisses me too hard like he doesn't know his own strength. His hands are running up and down my back, presumably in an attempt to increase my arousal but it really is not helping.

I don't feel relaxed enough and his timing is off; he's not sensitive to my slower pace and I feel that instead of bringing home an amorous and sexy young stud, I mistakenly got stuck with an excitable little puppy instead. Next thing I know, he picks me up in his arms and carries me towards the handful of stairs that lead to my bedroom.

He's not the strongest man in the world and in his head he probably thinks he has more strength because, as we climb the stairs, he totters wildly and I have to quickly pull my head back and practically strain my neck, in order to prevent it from getting banged up on the wall leading to my bedroom. Even though the door isn't fully opened, he gets my bedroom right, which is probably a fortunate guess on his part.

He rushes me to my bed and, before he totally drops me to the floor, he practically throws me on top of it and looks awfully relieved to have done so. He's so lucky my bedroom isn't at the end of the hall; he would never have made it. I am so *not* in the mood for sex right now and if I thought that it couldn't get any more comical, I was wrong. Standing at the side of my bed, looking and acting like a matador or something, he proceeds to undress.

Pulling off his shirt like maybe he's thinking that

he's a young Tom Cruise in Risky Business, he keeps his eyes fixed on me as if he's putting on a show. He obviously has some fantasy going on in his head and I'm wondering where the thoughtful and sensitive young man of earlier has gone off to just now. We spent the evening talking about how movies depict relationship as a fantasy that neither of us buy into and yet here he is... living proof that he doesn't know how to walk his talk.

"What are you doing?" I finally ask him as he kicks one of his shoes off and it hits my dresser so hard that it probably will leave a dent.

"What?" he asks, as if he just woke up from a sexy dream.

"We just spent the evening talking about movies and fantasies and how unreal movie sex is and yet, here you are, acting out... movie sex."

"This is movie sex?" he asks, looking totally confused and at sea.

"Don't get me wrong," I say softly, trying not to hurt his feelings, "I do want to make love to you, Martin. But I want it to be real."

"I wasn't being real?" he asks, sounding hurt.

"You weren't being sensitive to where I'm at... You weren't connecting with me; it was more like you were playing out a fantasy in your head, like you were putting on a performance instead of being present with me, here and now."

"Wow," he says petulantly, like I just slapped him hard in the face. "Nothing like a harsh critic to brutally bash opening night performance," he says as he looks for his shoe and puts back on his clothes.

"Where are you going?" I ask him, feeling awful but not knowing how to make this right.

"The mood's broken," he says as he looks

underneath the dresser, still trying to locate his wayward shoe. "I'm going to leave while I still have a semblance of male ego left."

Still half-dressed, he finds his shoe and a few seconds later, I hear the front door close; Martin has left the building.

CHAPTER 8

I sleep like crap and when I wake up I'm feeling like I have a terrible hangover, even though I hardly drank much at all. I have so many mixed feelings about the previous evening but mostly anger seems the predominant emotion although self-recrimination is running a close second.

Why did I take Martin home with me last night? What was I thinking? Obviously, I wasn't thinking. What was *he* thinking with the whole strip tease act in my bedroom? Did he think that I'd find his dorky gyrations sexy or a big come on? Has his act worked with any other women? Is it me? Am I out of touch? Should I have just gone along with it so as not to have him flip out on me like he did? Was I being insensitive to his insensitivity of me?

As I put on the water for my morning coffee, I once again swear off men and dating; it's just not worth the upset and endless self-questioning. I'm never going to figure out how to have a successful man-woman relationship so I might as well admit defeat and give up trying. How many times can a heart get broken, anyway? Anybody ever done a study on that? If so, I'd like to see those results.

As I open the fridge to get the milk my face suddenly breaks out into a smile when I realize that Martin must have thought he was Richard Gere when he graduates as an officer and carries Debra Winger out of her lousy conveyer-belt job in the very last scene of *An Officer and a Gentleman*. That was a classic moment, I have to admit but it was a friggin' movie, for crying out loud.

My cell phone rings and I see right away that it's Janice. I hesitate because I have to ask myself if I'm ready for our usual disagreeable conversation this early in the day. I take the call anyway, because she's my daughter and I've never blown her off, ever. Besides, maybe today is the day we have a wonderful conversation and I'll feel like Mother of the Year afterwards. I'm in a goofball mood today, I notice.

"Hey, Janice. What's up?"

"Grammy called me and wanted to know if I was going to her thing," she says and stops.

"Her birthday, yeah," I say, expecting her to say more. "So, you're going?"

"I told her I'd be going up with you," she says and I'm still not clear on the purpose of her call.

"Yeah, we talked about that, right?" I ask.

"Just want to make sure," she says and I'm still not getting her drift.

"You want to make sure that I'm going?" I ask, sounding cheerful and hoping not to sound condescending at any point, which is one of her major accusations lately.

"I didn't tell you for sure I was going last time, so, I guess, I told grammy I'd go, so I guess, I'm definitely going, with you, I guess," she says and I have to wonder how she's getting on in college with such limited command of the English language.

"I'm happy to hear that you're definitely going," I say. "I'll pick you up on the way. We'll have a great time," I say with as much cheer as I can muster.

"Yeah," she says lamely and I wonder to myself if she's deliberately trying to deflate my positive buzz.

"Is everything else going well?" I ask. "How are your studies going?"

"Okay, I guess. I've been editing the short that we just shot, me and Jane. It's my movie but she's been helping out, with the acting and stuff."

"That's terrific. I can't wait to see it."

"You won't like it, mom. It's kinda like political and stuff."

"I didn't know you were that political, sweetie. You were never…"

"It's not political like about current politics and all that Republican, Democrat bullshit… it's about sexual politics and all the sexual discrimination and stuff that nobody wants to talk about."

"Oh, good," I say and I instantly know that I'm sounding like an out-of-touch mom that doesn't understand her daughter's head space, at all. "That sounds really interesting."

"I just need to get a good grade; it's not like I'm using it to get funding to make a full feature like some of the other students. I should say *many* of the students because that's what most of them are there for; to try and get a career out of it, in Hollywood."

I restrain myself from asking her exactly why is she going to film school and why she doesn't see it as a direct route to Hollywood but I feel like I'm on thin ice and I don't want to ruin a good conversation by asking any direct questions that might make her feel uncomfortable. I'm not going to understand her anyway, so I may as well try not to rock the boat. "As long as you're getting something out of it, that's the main thing, right?"

"I guess," she says and I can tell that she wants to go.

"I appreciate the call, sweetie and I'm really looking forward to seeing you… will I be seeing you before the trip?"

"I don't think so, mom. Things are really busy, right now."

"Fair enough. I hope you're getting enough rest and

everything."

"Yes, mom. Gotta go."

"Love you," I say but I'm not sure if she heard me or maybe she was hanging up while I was saying it but it would have been nice to hear her say it back.

Ronald hasn't gotten back to me about the sketches so I don't want to work on anything new until I hear from him. I could call him and ask but, seriously, I hate the project and if I can put it off for a few more days... that will suit me just fine. I should stop being lazy and do some yoga. My ass is feeling like a big bucket of dough this morning.

Just as I'm stretching into the downward-facing dog yoga pose, my phone rings. It's not playing *Good Vibrations* or any of my familiar, friends and family ring tones so I assume that it must be work-related. It's a local number that I don't recognize so I pause the yoga DVD and take the call, "Hello?"

"Is this Frances?" a male voice asks.

"Yes," I answer, my memory banks unsuccessfully trying to match a name to the voice.

"This is Jonathan... from Café Luna," he says and a cold shudder runs up my spine. "I'm John at work and Jonathan when I'm not at the restaurant," he clarifies, perhaps assuming that my silence has more to do with faulty recognition than with outright shock. I guess he got my business card, after all.

"How are you?" he asks.

"Fine," I answer, still trying to get my bearings.

"Is it okay for me to call you? I know it's been a few days..."

"No, that's fine. I'm sorry, I wasn't expecting... I was in the middle of doing yoga, actually..."

"Well, I won't keep you. I thought maybe you'd like to meet me for dinner tonight?" he says.

"No, I'm sorry," I say, anxious to get off the phone. "I can't tonight."

John the waiter pauses before he speaks, as if perhaps thinking to himself that he wasn't expecting such a brush off. "Do you have plans for lunch today?" he asks.

I don't want to go to lunch with him but I don't want to lie, either.

"Let me take you out for lunch, then," he says, taking my silence as a no.

"I'm not sure how the day..." I begin to say, part of me saying that my day is wide open and what's the harm of meeting the guy for lunch?

"I can do noon or one o'clock. What's the best time for you?" he interrupts.

"Noon is probably best," I say.

"Terrific," he says quickly. "Want to meet me at the Urth Café on Main or should I come pick you up?"

"I can meet you there," I say.

"Excellent. I look forward to it. See you at noon, then," he says and hangs up. Wow, that was... what just happened? I just agreed to meet John the waiter for lunch is what happened. I had no intentions of going out with the guy but I have to hand it to him... what a smooth operator.

I finish out the yoga program but my mind isn't really in it as all I keep thinking to myself is what an odd turn my life has been taking lately. I've got two young guys interested in me and I'm not even sure if I'm interested in them back.

I know I'm not faultless in the whole situation and parts of me find it amusing and exciting but a large part of me is feeling terrified and I'm not sure which part of me will be the eventual winner. I'll just have to see how it goes. I'm almost forty and I guess I'm still a desirable hot Chiquita, after all, I smile to myself. Now, what am I going to wear?

John the waiter sits waiting for me under one of the large umbrellas that shield the café patio. Urth Café attracts the upscale chic and trendy and John the waiter, or I should say, Jonathan, fits right in. It's strange seeing him outside of the restaurant and even though he's wearing casual clothes, he still looks clean, crisp and fine. He gently rises from his chair and kisses my cheek as if he's greeting me aboard his multi-million dollar yacht.

"You look fantastic," he says and I instantly feel fantastic, just because he told me so. "Are you hungry?"

I don't know what it is but the effect this guy has on me... I feel like saying that I'm ravenous and I could eat him up, right here, right now... but instead I act demurely and delicately open up the menu as if to glance at their tasty offerings. "I am feeling a bit peckish," I say and it would appear that I am now an English lady sitting on the veranda of her country estate, meeting Sir Jonathan for high tea.

"I'm so glad you agreed to meet with me," he says with that million dollar smile of his. As he beams it in my direction I only now realize that I actually missed seeing it. Whatever it is about sexual energy—I couldn't even begin to understand how it all works—this guy has it in spades. Does he have this effect on all women or is it just me?

"I'm delighted that you invited me," I answer and I casually look around to see if any women are looking over to check him out. "I love this little café and I don't get invited here as often as I'd like," I say and it seems that my English lady character wants to be doing all the talking.

"Did I tell you how amazing you're looking today?" he asks and I feel like shielding my face with the open menu because I know my face is blushing madly.

"You're such a charmer, aren't you?" I admonish, without any bite. "I'll bet you can get any girl that you want."

"I may try and have some success," he says, "but at the end of the day, the heart wants what the heart wants."

I can feel my heart go a fluttering when he looks into my eyes and says that with such an earnest and devoted expression upon his face. Although a part of me wants to believe him, another part of me is wondering what school for scoundrels this young man graduated from.

"What are you having to eat?" I ask, hoping to nip this seduction in the bud and lower my heart beat to a more normal level of functioning.

"Something light," he says, finally shifting his penetrating gaze off my face and back to the menu. "I may have a salad."

Wow, a guy that eats salads, that's a first. Is he watching his figure? His body does look really fit and, what's the word... svelte.

"What about you?" he asks and for some reason his question spooks me and I get flustered.

"What?" I ask.

"To eat," he says, smiling. "What are you having to eat?"

"Oh," I say, looking quickly down at the menu and feeling pressured like I have to have my mind made up on some food that I wasn't even thinking about... "Salad sounds good," I quickly say, as if I'm on a game show and I answered just before the buzzer sounded.

"Cool," he says and lowers his menu to adore me with his eyes all over again. Oh lord, I don't think I'm going to survive this lunch.

When Jonathan is not giving disarming compliments, he surprises me as being a thoughtful person with ideas that he doesn't seem to have borrowed from the consensus of public opinion. He's a wonderful conversationalist and our time together flows smoothly. He tells me that he's an aspiring director but he does act and write as well. In LA parlance, like most wannabe creative individuals, he's considered a hyphenate: actor-writer-director. He's still gazing deeply into my eyes as we finish our salads and agree that we're too full for dessert.

"I also paint," he says. "Not to sell, though. I paint just for me."

"That's fantastic," I say and all of a sudden I'm feeling like I'm a total slacker.

"Would you like to see my paintings?" he asks as I put enough cash on the payment wallet to pay for my meal.

"I'd love to... what, you mean now?" I ask, checking my watch as if time was an issue for me. "Are they in a gallery?" I ask innocently.

"No," he smiles. "I told you that I don't sell them. I live within walking distance."

He's inviting me back to his place? I don't think so.

"That's very nice of you, Jonathan but some other time, okay?" I say, standing as if I'm already late for something.

"You could see my painting of you," he then says and I stand stock still and feel a little thrill of energy that makes me feel secretly, wildly pleased. In this moment, Jonathon seems so authentic and vulnerable and when he gives me that million dollar smile of his, I melt a little bit.

"You have a painting of me?" I ask, a tad breathlessly.

"It's just your face. You have the beautiful kind of face that painter's love to paint," he says, or words to that effect, my thoughts were actually all scrambled as he is talking. No one's ever painted me before. He did say it was my face and not some nude fantasy that he's got going on. Is my face really that... paintable?

"I live just two blocks away. I really want to know what you think," he insists.

"Okay," I say, as if everything pressing in my life is now… un-pressed. "Just very briefly," I say weakly, unable to fully process that a stranger has actually painted my portrait.

Jonathan's place is a really cute little pad above a gift store on a side street off Main street. It's not cluttered like most bachelor pads I've seen; in fact, I'm impressed by how clean and neat it is.

"Red or white?" he asks, holding aloft two bottles of wine, one in each hand.

"Oh, I don't have time… I'm not…"

"If I remember correctly, you only drink red," he says, smiling.

"I sometimes drink white," I argue.

"Would you prefer white?" he asks.

"No, red is fine," I say and as he goes to his small kitchen to open it, I look around for my painting. I'm surprised that I don't see *any* paintings; on my way here I had a picture of an artist's loft with easels and canvasses and lots of work in progress. I can't even get a whiff of the characteristic smell of oil-based paints. It doesn't seem like there's been any painting going on in here, period.

"Do you have a studio or do you do your painting here?" I ask as he returns with a large glass of wine.

"I paint here, mostly," he says casually. "Take a seat," he says, indicating a love seat which he sits down upon.

"Where's the painting?" I ask, sitting down on the edge of the love seat.

"I'll get it in a minute," he says. "I had a really nice time with you."

"I had a nice time with you, too," I answer.

"How is the wine?"

"It's good, thank you."

"You have such beautiful hair," he says, brushing my hair lightly with his hand, which actually feels really nice. It's been so long since I was touched by a man. "I liked you the first time I laid eyes upon you."

"You did?" I ask, taking another sip of wine.

"It felt like I knew you already, like we had an instant connection," he says and I hesitate to agree for fear of giving him the impression that I'm interested. I don't know what's going on with my body but every time he runs his hand through my hair, it's like I get a rush of adrenalin and my heart beats a little faster. I try to control it but it's doesn't seem to help, at all.

"Do you believe in people having an instant connection?" he asks.

"Sure, yes, of course."

"Why do you say, of course?" he asks calmly.

"I just mean that there's some people you can click with right away and others, not so much," I say and I'm wondering why my thoughts are feeling so scrambled.

"Would you say that we clicked right away?" he asks with a devious grin on his face. I only imagine it's a devious grin because I'm actually afraid of turning around and looking directly at him. I feel like if I allowed myself to totally relax and lean back on his love seat as he caresses my hair and face... let's just say that this is definitely a slippery slope that I'm on, here.

"I would have to say that you would be one of the many people in my life, in my experience, whom I have felt more comfortable with, as against not so much comfortable with," I say and even I make a squishy face wondering to myself what on earth I'm babbling on about. "There really is no painting, is there?" I then boldly ask, hoping to put an end to this whole charade or attempted seduction or whatever it is.

"Of course there's a painting. I'll go get it," he says and quickly jumping up, he goes over to and opens what appears to be a closet door in the small hallway. After rooting around in the closet for a bit, he comes back with a small, maybe 10 x 14, stretched canvas which he places on the seat of a straight-backed chair.

"It's a work in progress, you understand," he says nervously. "And bear in mind that I was painting it from memory."

The portrait is indeed only half-finished and it looks nothing like me. The nose is too big, the hair is too long and I do not have such high cheekbones. In fairness, he was painting from memory and I don't want to tell him how inaccurate it the whole thing is.

"You hate it," he says, standing back, as if terrified of my verdict.

"No, I don't hate it at all," I insist. "It just doesn't... look very much like me."

"Well, maybe someday you can pose for me and I can... get it right?" he asks hopefully.

"I really don't think..." I say and I'm not sure what to say.

"Stand up," he says, holding his hands out for me to grab hold of, which I do. I may have stood up too fast as I'm feeling a bit dizzy and I end up standing closer to him than I had intended. He keeps hold of my right hand and with his right hand, he strokes my face, as maybe a painter would; looking at me as if he was sketching me in his mind.

"You have perfect symmetry," he says, "in your face... and your cheekbones are so refined and... delicate."

Despite the fact that I know that he's being cheesy, I still find myself blushing coyly like a teenager. As he leans in closer, I know that I should turn my head to avoid his kiss but for some strange reason, after I make a note to myself to ask Dr. Roberts about this later, I'm feeling helpless, hopeless and lost in such close proximity to him. Everything about this man is such a hot turn on for me that I'm beginning to question my sanity.

As his lips get closer, I can feel a hot rush course through every cell in my body. His lips pass my lips, however and even though I didn't really want him to kiss me, my body feels cheated. I can feel his hot breath on my cheek as his mouth glides past and lingers just centimeters from my ear.

"Not even DaVinci or Botticelli could do your beauty justice," he whispers and something about the way he pronounces 'Botticelli' causes a heat to rise and spread throughout me and my body just then decides to give itself to him. Please now kiss me my body pleads to him and my personality apparently can see no reason to resist.

Time seems to have slowed down. I still feel his hot breath on my cheek, as if his lips are waiting patiently for a positive gesture from me. I sense his moist lips as they remain poised, as if lingering with intent. I sense that he will not move forward until he receives a clear signal from me that I am in agreement. I know that he's waiting.

All I have to do is turn my head slightly towards him and our lips will touch and in this moment... I want nothing else. As I turn my face, ever so slowly, I feel almost intoxicated by his scent. It's not the pungent odor of cologne or anything artificial... it's his natural body aroma and I feel my lungs breathing more deeply to suck every molecule of that scent in. Whatever pheromones this man is emitting, they are waking parts of my brain and body that has been asleep for such a very long time.

"Kiss me," I hear myself say and as if that was

exactly the invitation he was waiting for, his head turns ever so slowly towards mine and our lips caress ever so softly. For such a soft and tender kiss, it sends huge aftershocks throughout my entire system; from my lips the shock waves shudder all the way down to the tips of my toes.

As he kisses me more deeply now, my body begins to feel like warm jelly and I can feel my knees buckle. As if the excitement is too much to bear, something in me panics and I quickly pull back. I bump against the chair and the painting gets knocked to the floor. As if the thud of the painting hitting the floor breaks whatever spell I'm in, I feel suddenly like I'm back in the here and now and all I can feel is a terror dancing ugly in my chest.

"What is it?" he asks softly.

I'm not sure how to answer as even I am never quite sure what is going on in my unfathomable head and heart. "I'm just feeling a bit… maybe some water?" I say, perhaps hoping that I would feel better if he could give me some space.

"Yes, of course," he says and as he goes to the kitchen, I do feel better, as if now I can breathe. I bend down to pick up the painting and I notice a name handwritten on the back of the canvas. I have to focus hard to decipher if indeed it is a name. When I do, I get a cold wet shock of sober reality slap me hard in the face.

"Who's Marguerite?" I ask as he returns with a glass of water. He stops cold in his step and looks at me as if his mind is trying to decode how I came up with that name. When he sees the painting in my hand, he instantly knows.

"Marguerite is… was an old college…" he says and stops when he sees me head straight out the door. "Frances, wait!" he calls but I don't turn back.

Jonathan catches up with me on the street as I walk hurriedly towards my car.

"Frances, I can explain," he says.

"You're such a liar," I say, barely able to look at him.

"No, I'm not," he argues. "I was going to turn the painting into you."

"You were going to turn a painting of your ex-girlfriend into me?" I say, hoping he would see the ridiculousness of his logic.

"It's just a painting. She means nothing to me... please stop and let's talk about this," he says and runs in front of me to block me from opening the door of my car. "Okay, so I lied about the painting. I made that up to help you out," he says.

"You lied to help *me* out?" I ask with a good measure of WTF in my voice.

"You wouldn't have come up, otherwise, would you?" he asks.

"No, I would not," I answer, hoping to sound impatient as well as annoyed.

"Well, look, the painting is like a cup of coffee, right?" he says.

"What?"

"Have you never invited someone up to your apartment for a cup of coffee?" he asks. "But you don't really mean coffee, right? We say coffee to make the other person feel comfortable about saying yes... that's what I was doing with you. We were at a coffee shop so I couldn't ask you up for coffee, could I? So instead of coffee I said painting. In my father's day, they used to ask women up to see their etchings... seriously," he says and right when he says the word 'etchings,' I snigger, which surprises me. I don't feel any better so I'm figuring that the snigger is coming from nervousness rather than from a place of fun.

"I understand that you were feeling awkward," he continues, "and I wanted to give you the best reason I could think of for saying yes. I'm sorry that I lied."

"I'm sorry too, Jonathan. I'm sure that you're a really nice person but I'm just not into playing games."

"So, you want to make me the bad guy here," he says, looking hurt, "and what, you want to play the innocent victim?"

"Please let me leave," I say.

"If all of this is a mistake..." he says, pausing to find the right words. "Are you telling me that this is all me?" he asks.

"That what is all you?"

"This," he says. "You and me. Are you telling me that you don't feel a connection between us? It's only me that feels it... is that what you're telling me?"

"Jonathan, please... I just want to go..."

"Why did you keep coming back to the restaurant? Why do you look at me the way that you do? Why did you give me your phone number? Why did you come meet me for lunch? Why did you come up to my apartment?"

He waits for me to answer but I don't really have one.

"Oh, that's right." he says. "You don't play games."

As he walks back to his apartment, I don't know whether to call him back or run after him or do nothing and let him walk out of my life. I'm so conflicted and confused; all I really want to do is get into my car and drive home to safety.

As I drive back to my apartment, it doesn't take too long for tears to begin streaming down my face. I don't care that I'm tearing up and that my body is shaking from the intensity of my sobbing; what bothers me the most is not that I'm crying but that I don't know why.

CHAPTER 9

"A lot can happen in your world in just one short week," Dr. Roberts says and I can almost sense her licking her mental chops. My therapy sessions for the past while must have been quite boring for her, with them mostly consisting of me talking about missing-wanting-hating Bill, never wanting to date again, near constant whinging about aging, how much I hate my life, how difficult my daughter is, and so forth. I'm sure I must have sounded like a broken record after not too long.

"How does it make you feel to have two different men interested in you after such a long time of abstinence?" she asks.

"Mixed feelings," I answer, trying to internally search for my most predominant ones. "It's certainly nice to feel attractive and desirable, I won't lie," I say, thoughtfully. "But I'm also feeling like I could make a terrible mistake and... I feel very confused, mainly," I finally answer.

"What's confusing for you?" she asks.

"All of it," I quickly reply. "They each bring up so many different feelings inside me that... I don't even know what I'm feeling, half the time. I'm more physically attracted to Jonathan, for instance yet being in his presence terrifies me whereas with Martin I feel safer, more myself but less, I don't know... sexy."

"What is it about Jonathan that terrifies you, do you think?"

"He's... um, I'm so... Our connection is so, uh, sexual or maybe primal or something, more visceral, I guess. It's like he's my New York and Martin is my Santa Monica

Beach," I explain, referring to the analogy I told her about earlier. "Except that if I stay in New York for very long I get burned out and the desire to be there dies and if I stay on the beach for too long... I get bored."

"I see," Dr. Roberts says, sensing that I have more in the tank.

"Jonathan plays games... like, he's a player... but then again, he can be so earnest and solemn, also. Martin doesn't play games and I can really communicate with him on a mental level and he really listens and he looks like he's trying so hard... but the sexual overtures that he made were awful and I don't think I can have a relationship with someone I can't connect with, sexually. Jonathan blows me away sexually, almost like it's too much and I can feel my brain and my thoughts get all scrambled just by being around him..." I sputter on and stop as if I'm feeling mentally exhausted.

"Okay," Dr. Roberts says, as if it's her way of saying, 'time out.' "Would you agree that it's too early to tell just exactly what your relationship could be with each of these gentlemen? You barely know either of them, wouldn't you say?"

"Yes, of course."

"So, a lot of what you think about them is speculation and some measure of projection on your part, which is only natural, of course."

"Yes."

"As relationships evolve and we get to spend more time with a person, our confusion about them lessens; the more we get to know them and find out who they truly are, then we can best determine what role is appropriate for them to play in our lives."

"Yes."

"Your confusion is natural at such an early stage but

what I'm sensing from you the most are your own fears. Your responses to meeting both these men almost borders on panic on your part, would you agree?"

"I guess."

"We can speculate all we want about who these men really are and what they may or may not be thinking but that would be wasted time or our part, agreed?" she asks and I nod, yes.

"What we can take a look at are your feelings and your responses to meeting these men and how you are being affected by your relationship to them, you see?"

"Yes. Of course."

"Tell me why you fear that you'll make a terrible mistake?" she then asks.

"Well, I guess, I'm afraid that if I choose wrong or make a bad decision that it could be a big mistake."

"And?" she prompts.

"And I'll get hurt and end up regretting it afterwards."

"So, you're afraid of moving forward for fear of getting hurt and feeling regret for making a bad decision?"

"That's... only natural, isn't it?" I ask, secretly feeling like an emotional wuss.

"Yes, it is only too natural, especially when one has been hurt in a similar situation before. Fear is designed to play a healthy role in our lives. If we have put our hand in a fire and been burned before, the resulting fear we have of fire is a healthy one, wouldn't you say? The fear we now have of fire prevents us from being careless and putting our hand back in and of being burned in the future."

"Exactly," I agree.

"However, fear can also play an unhealthy role in our lives if it prevents us from moving forward into what I would call a growth situation for ourselves."

"So, in my situation, I have an unhealthy fear?" I ask.

"Let me give you a for instance…" she says and I relax more as she begins. As usual, when I ask Dr. Roberts whether she thinks something I'm doing is the right thing or the wrong thing, rather than tell me a straight yes or no, she'll often give me a 'for instance.'

"I had a client that didn't know that he had a certain fear until his new wife had a hot tub installed in their house. It became a problem for them when he would always have an excuse not to join her in the hot tub: the water was too hot, the jets were too strong, he was tired, he had too much work to do and so on.

"When we took a look at his attitudes to water in general, he described himself as a 'shower rather than a bath person.' He didn't like the ocean and would sit by the side of a swimming pool but never be tempted to actually swim in one. When he did try to sit in the hot tub with his wife, he said that after a few minutes he felt panic and assumed that the temperature or some other feature of the tub was affecting him adversely."

"He had a fear of water?" I ask.

"Our analysis eventually uncovered some childhood trauma associated with being given baths by the household nanny when he was a toddler. When she bathed him, she was very rough and on several occasions would dunk his head in the water so that it felt to him like he was drowning. Although he had forgotten about these events, the fear remained in his unconscious and became active every time he was faced with immersing himself in a body of water."

"He avoided water all his life and he didn't even know that he was afraid of it?" I ask, incredulously.

"If you avoid what you're fearful of, you wouldn't know that you have a fear, would you? It's only when you hit up against something that you're fearful of... that you recognize, that, oh yes, I'm feeling fearful."

"Okay, so in my situation... I have fears around relationship that I didn't know I had until I started going back on dates again?"

"One of the most predominant fears we all have... and to my knowledge, there are no exclusions, except maybe the Dalai Lama or someone... are fears centered around intimacy. This planet would be a completely different one if we didn't all have a fear of intimacy. So, don't feel bad, you're not alone, by any stretch."

"So, when I kissed Jonathan and felt a panic, it didn't mean that he was bad for me and that the situation was all wrong... I was hitting up against my own fear?"

"Correct. Now, that's not to say that the situation may or may not be wrong for you, only you can determine that but ninety-nine percent of the time, your panic indicates unresolved trauma that needs to be addressed for continued growth to occur."

"I see," I say, thoughtfully.

As I drive back home, I'm not thinking about me and Jonathan and Martin; I'm thinking about the man and his fear of open water (if indeed someone like that actually exists as, for all the 'for instances' that Dr. Roberts gives, I really think that some of my therapist's anecdotal stories, if not all of them, are made up entirely for my benefit).

In any event, I could imagine the man, in various situations in his life, choosing not to take a bath or refraining from swimming in the ocean and here's the kicker: he didn't even know why.

I could imagine him going to Vegas with his buddies and sitting by the pool while the rest of the guys splashed around in the pools and the hot tubs and asking him why he wasn't joining them. I imagined all the excuses he would tell them like he didn't want to get his hair wet or maybe he was afraid of getting an ear infection or something but what I find truly fascinating is that the excuses he was making up were for real. It wasn't that he was thinking up random excuses to give for not swimming; he actually *believed* the excuses himself.

If he never had someone close to him insist that he share a hot tub with them... he could have lived his whole life without having taken a swim in the ocean... ever. Wow.

Okay, so if I apply this 'for instance' to my own life, what am I avoiding and making excuses to myself for not doing? If I narrow it down to relationships... I've been avoiding getting involved with someone for all these years because I'm afraid of being hurt. Well, at least it's not brain science... that one's pretty easy to work out. What about all the fears that I don't know about that's keeping me from doing stuff or, as Dr. Roberts would say, keeping me from 'moving forward in my life in order for growth to occur?' Maybe when I get home, I should make a list.

As I get in the front door of my apartment, my cell phone rings: it's Ronald.

"Hello, Ronald, what's going on?" I answer.

"Busy, busy," he answers. "It's all good."

"That's great."

"I just sent you an email and it explains everything but I wanted to tell you personally how pleased I am with your work."

"Thank you."

"They loved all of your ideas and they want to go with sketch 201. I made detailed notes in the email."

"Terrific."

"How are things with you?" he asks.

"Good. I'm looking forward to my mom's birthday

party."

"That's at the weekend, right? She lives in San Rafael County, doesn't she?"

"Yes and yes... why do you ask?"

"That's not far from where Frank lives," he says and I'm not sure where he's going with this. "I'll be up there this weekend."

"You should move up there at this stage," I say.

"It would be great to be able to invite him to something. I'm always going to his things and I'd really like you to meet him."

"You want to bring him to my mom's birthday party?"

"Unless it's an intrusion. We could just swing by and make a field trip out of it, stay at a local B&B. It'll be a good excuse to get him out of the city."

"You're welcome to come, sure. As long as you don't mind talking to old folks; it'll be mostly my mom's friends and some of them are getting up there."

"That's not a problem, at all. I love old people."

"Okay. Sure, I'd love to meet Frank. I'll email you the details."

"Super," he says and we hang up. Did he just say that he loves old people?

When I check his email and take a closer look at the design they want, I realize that it requires more work than Ronald suggested on the phone. The notes are hard to follow and a lot of them are abstract like, 'the shapes chosen should conform in some way to the mental state of Therese, which could be described as puzzled, ragged or jagged; hence uneven, raggedy surfaces should predominate over straight lines, curves or circles and so on.'

As I pour myself a glass of wine and sit down to look over the text one more time, I wonder about the mental

107

state of Therese. I wonder what it would take for her to resolve the relationships in her life and move forward to the heaven part. I compare her situation to mine and then wonder about my own unresolved relationships.

If I was being honest with myself I'd have to admit that pretty much every relationship in my life is 'unresolved.' I find this fact shocking to the point of thinking that maybe I ought to be doing something about it. If the author is saying that if we have unresolved issues in our lives and therefore, our souls don't move on when we die... then I'm in serious doo-doo.

I could make a list but I already know all the players, starting with both my parents. Last that I heard, my father is in Colorado having started a brand new family. I haven't wanted to talk to him since, well, since he had enough of my mother and rode off into the sunset. As for my mother, I've barely spoken much to her since Janice was born... and as for Janice? What is her deal, anyway?

My sister Doris and I hardly ever speak, except around Thanksgiving and birthdays. Why are we not more sisterly towards each other? Sure, she lives up near mom still but what unresolved issues do we have? I was considered the pretty one and she always seemed jealous of me but that's hardly my fault or responsibility.

Then there are all the men in my life: Jim Costas, the creep who bailed on me and never even wanted to know his own daughter. Maybe Janice blames me for that; if the right moment comes along, I should ask her.

Steve is back in my life, after a long absence. I can't blame Steve for anything; I did leave him for Bill, after all. I never did apologize to him for all the hurt I've caused him so definitely I could do some serious apology work there and maybe consider one relationship resolved, yay.

As for Bill... I wouldn't know where to start. I have

so many unanswered questions to ask him that it would probably take forever to resolve that one; not that I'm even going to get the chance.

Maybe the focus should not be on resolving old relationships that can't be fixed but I should make sure that present and future ones don't get messed up, instead. I think Ronald and I are just fine. He's so self-obsessed, it's a totally one-way relationship, anyway; so as long as he's not much interested in my private life, I'm pretty much safe.

As much as I have a hard time not thinking about him, I'm going to discount Jonathan as having any kind of relationship with me, period. He's a player and a manipulator and he's just plain old trouble, if you ask me. Let that guy even slightly in and I know it could only end up in heartache.

Martin, on the other hand, is a sweetheart. When I think of him, I smile and I get a warm feeling in my heart. He's goofy and funny and he may not be as hip and trendy as he thinks he is but he means well. The sex thing is a big problem. I know that sexual compatibility is majorly important but I also know that it's too soon to tell and differences in styles can be worked out, if both parties are willing (which, luckily, he seems to be).

I have some books on my bookshelf left over from the 'Bill won't touch me' days where I tried to get Bill interested enough to try out some things, which he never found the time for. I found the Kama Sutra really interesting but the book all about Tantric Sex would probably help Martin and I.

As far as I can tell, Tantric Sex is not about getting it on just so that you can experience an orgasm at the end of your exertions but rather based upon the idea that the journey *is* the destination. It's all about being in the moment and being sensitive to your own and the other person's 'energy.' Even if half of it is BS, just the idea of taking it slow is a good idea to start with for us both.

That's assuming, of course, that Martin is actually still interested. It's been several days since our disaster in the bedroom and I'm beginning to wonder if he's ever going to call me again. Guys can be very sensitive about their sexual abilities and maybe my comments really struck a nerve and chased him away, for good. Great, add one more unresolved relationship to the list. If I don't hear from him, maybe I should call him in a bit, apologize if I was being insensitive and at least, get some closure or whatever.

Thanks to this awful French play from a century ago, I could be looking at the new me.

Instead of working some more on the Therese project, I decide to chill out with another glass of vino and curl up on the bed with the Zen book. The more I get into it, the more I like. The problem I have found with self-help books, however, is that the authors usually make everything sound simple as pie, as if everything they were talking about was just plain common sense. Of course, couples should have clear communication at all times; certainly, resentments have a tendency to grow out of proportion, when not addressed; absolutely, telling lies and playing games is no way to build up trust between people, duh.

What I do like about the Zen book is that there are clear exercises to follow and it even devotes a chapter to Zen in the bedroom, which I've already highlighted to the point that nearly every other line is now yellow. There is an exercise I know already that I want to try with Martin. It involves standing naked facing each other and instead of seeing each other as purely sexual beings, we explore each other's body with our finger tips. As if all our concentration was focused on the tips of our fingers, we stroke each other's bodies in a non-sexual way.

It suggests that two people can attain greater intimacy this way rather than going the direct route of getting naked and jumping each other's bones; I'm paraphrasing, of course. The exercises actually sound like a lot of fun and even if the intention is not to get turned on, I'm pretty aroused right now just reading about our bare finger tips stroking our naked bodies all over the place. Maybe it's the few glasses of wine and this non-sexy, sexy book but I'm feeling definitely horny. I should call Martin and see what he's up to.

"Hello," he answers and right off, I can tell that he's nervous.

"Hello, Martin," I say and I'm wondering if he even knows that it's me calling.

"I'm sorry for leaving like that," he says and I can't help myself but I love a man that can say, 'I'm sorry.'

"I'm sorry for being so insensitive," I say and by the way the conversation is going, I know that we're not done with each other. "I had a lovely evening."

He asks me what I'm doing and I tell him about the Zen book I'm reading. Once again he surprises me and rather than dismissing my reading as something only a woman would read and changing the topic, he actually asks me questions about Zen and relationship. His sensitivity and his curiosity cheers me and makes me feel hopeful about us.

As we talk some more, I begin to miss him. When he says that he'd love to try the exercise with me, I actually think about inviting him over. The episode with Jonathan is still too fresh in my mind, though, so I quickly dismiss the thought. However, I do invite him to my mother's birthday, which takes us both by surprise. He sounds down on the phone and with me being away, I didn't want to go so many days without seeing him. I think he will fit in nicely with my kooky family and being out of LA could be really good for us both.

I say a quick goodbye to Martin when a call comes in from Ronald. Just as I'm about to take Ronald's call, I put him through to voicemail instead because I don't want anything to break the mood I've established with Martin. I want to think some more about our trip away together and if I mentally imagine what it will be like, I feel that I can quickly isolate some problem spots and call it off before it gets too advanced.

Part of me also doesn't want to think about Jonathan and I secretly don't trust myself to leave myself alone for too long. I've had such a great time with Martin so far and when I've been with him, I didn't think about anyone or anything else. It's a win-win for both of us, I think and the only downer I can think of right now is how Janice is going to take the news that she'll be sharing the ride to my mother's with my newest best man-friend.

CHAPTER 10

"I have to share the ride up with who?" Janice asks when I finally get the courage to call her the next day.

"Martin. His name is Martin. He's a really neat kid, guy, and I think you guys will really get along. He's a photographer."

"A photographer of what?"

"I don't know. He's freelance."

"He does like weddings and stuff?"

"I think he does do weddings and other freelance work, sure."

"Mom, I'm in film school and you think that I'm going to get along with your pal the wedding photographer? Do you even hear yourself talk sometimes?"

"I just thought that because he's closer to your age and, I don't know, he's a cool guy, that's all. You'll like him. He's a likable guy," I say and I don't really know what I'm saying or why I'm feeling so defensive.

"What do you mean he's closer to my age? How old is he?" Janice asks and I don't know how to answer. "How young is your new man friend, mom?"

"I think he's somewhere around in his twenties somewhere, I should ask him."

"Are you shitting me? In his twenties? Seriously? I'm in my twenties."

"You just turned twenty. Besides, age isn't important. I'm surprised that you of all people... would make an issue out of it."

"My mom's bonking a twenty-year-old. Excuse me while I throw up."

"So, anyway, it will be the three of us," I say, hoping to end the call.

"I don't think so, mom."

"Why? Are you discriminating against... age?"

"No, mom. I'm discriminating against you. This is so you to pull something like this."

"Something like what, exactly?"

"Once again, you only think about yourself. You never think about how you're affecting other people."

I take a deep breath to calm myself and I really do try to see things from her point of view. Practice Zen, practice Zen, I repeat to myself. "I thought that you'd be happy for me, supportive that I'm finally getting myself back out there," I say.

"No, mom, I'm not supportive of you getting back out there. I think that's the worst thing that you could possibly be doing."

"Why is that?"

"Okay, don't take this the wrong way but you're crazy enough being by yourself. When you get into a relationship, you get crazy times squared."

"What would you know what I'm like in relationship? You were just a girl when your dad left."

"First of all just because I called him dad, he's not my real dad and secondly, you think young girls are dumb and they don't have feelings? You think because I was young that I didn't know what was going on between you two; how you were driving him crazy half the time and you didn't even see how your self-obsessed... narcissism was pushing him away for all those years?"

Wow, I just about manage to say to myself; where is all this coming from? We've never talked about any of this before. What's been going on in that young head of hers... all this time?

"Janice, I don't know where all this is coming from but we obviously need to have a talk real soon. I'm sorry if you thought that I was acting crazy all the time and drove away your dad."

"He's not my dad!" Janice almost shouts, her patience apparently shot. "You drove away my real dad before I was even born! All you think about is yourself and how you miss your husband and all these years that you've been depressed and feeling sorry for yourself. Well, guess what? He *was* my dad and you're not the only one that misses him... that misses him all the time..." Janice pauses and I can hear her trying to hold back her sobs.

"Janice, you're right, we should have talked about this and..."

"It's a bit late now, isn't it? How can we talk about something when you've ruined my life already..." Janice says and I can hear her crying. "I can't get my childhood back, can I? The childhood that you so totally ruined."

"I'm so sorry that you feel that way, sweetheart. I never meant for you to..."

"I won't be riding up with you and your boyfriend so don't come pick me up," Janice says as I can tell that she's finished talking and wants to get off the phone.

"I understand, sweetie. Steve and Stacy are also going up if you want to catch..." I stop when I realize that she has hung up already. I still look at the phone in my hand to make sure that we're disconnected. I seem to be moving slowly as if I'm in shock, which I probably am. Accusing me of ruining her life is huge and I must take her seriously and not discount her feelings as being influenced by her studies or her friends or her relationship or some post-adolescent phase that she might be going through.

My daughter hates me and blames me for ruining her entire childhood. What do I do with that? If I took that on, the sheer weight of it and all its implications would crush me. What would Dr. Roberts say? She'd say that I can only be responsible for my own feelings and actions and shouldn't take responsibility for other people's feelings... but she's my daughter and what if the actions I took really did harm her in some irreparable way? I've been a lousy parent; that, I can readily admit.

I work hard on the play project and make all of their suggested changes. I'm beyond happy to email the final plans off and hopefully this will be the end of it.

I invite Steve over for lunch and because neither of us mentioned Stacy, I'm expecting him to come alone, which he does. "How is my favorite person doing today?" he greets me at the door with a mixed bouquet of flowers. I have to give credit to him; he never arrives someplace, empty-handed.

"If I'm your favorite person, your life must suck," I joke as I greet his cheek with a kiss. "I don't know what you're hungry for," I say as I lead him to the living room area where I've set out a spread on the coffee table. "I shouldn't be telling you this but I'm kinda using up everything in my fridge that might spoil while I'm out of town."

"That sounds delicious!" he mocks. "And you're right, you shouldn't have told me that."

"Don't worry, it's all good. There's some lovely cheeses and a mixed salad, of course; crackers, bread, fruit, these grapes are delicious... just no meat, sorry."

"It all looks wonderful," Steve says. "I came for the company, anyways. What's going on?"

I tell Steve about my project and we talk about his gallery for a bit...

"So you're bringing your boy toy to your mom's

birthday party?" Steve then asks, as if he couldn't wait for the subject to come up. "The young guy from the restaurant you told me about?" he says when I continue to look at him in puzzlement. "Janice called me and asked if I'd give her a ride."

"Oh," I say, seeing now how it all fits together.

"So, spill," he says, like a teenager. "You two are getting it on?"

"Jeez," I say, making a face like I just ate a sour lemon. "The sixties just called and they want their lingo back. 'Getting it on?'" I say.

"Tell me about him," he says, undeterred.

"He's..." I begin and stop, not really knowing how to describe him; at least, describe him to Steve, that is.

"He rocks your world?"

"I wouldn't say he rocks it; just a little shake and bake, maybe," I say, totally lost for words.

"Shake and bake? That doesn't sound like much of a connection," Steve says.

"Steve, I don't know how to talk to you about this. He's a neat guy who I seem to get along great with. He's terrific company and... I like who I am when I'm with him," I say, happy with myself for coming up with the last part.

"O-kay," Steve says, picking at the cheeses. "So it's more a friendship than a hot and heavy?"

"Steve, all due respect but even if it was a 'hot and heavy,' as you put it, I don't feel comfortable talking to you about that aspect of my life. No offence." Steve makes a 'peace' gesture as he takes a bite of cheese and crackers, crumbs going everywhere. "I would say, at this stage, that we are more friends than... jeez, lovers, I guess, for now."

"That's cool," Steve says. "It's important to be friends first."

"Yeah," I say, as I make a sandwich for myself.

117

"Stacy and me is hot and heavy," he says, crumbs dangling haphazardly on his new goatee.

"That's nice," I say, hoping to sound uninterested. "Would you like a glass of wine?" I ask, as if I just thought of something that should have been offered ages before.

"Love one," he answers. "Red or white, I don't care."

"Let me ask you something," I say, after we both had polished off two glasses of wine and having talked a bit more about relationships, in general.

"Shoot," he says.

"You never seemed to... hate me," I say.

"What now?" he asks, putting down his glass of wine.

"It can't have been easy for you... the hurt I must have caused you," I say as I search awkwardly for the right words. "I know there was a long gap in years since we saw each other again but... you still wanted to be my friend."

"I like you," he says, as if that explains everything. "Always have. I married you, didn't I?"

"Yes, but... I guess what I really want to say to you is that... I'm sorry."

Steve looks at me like I've suddenly morphed into a different person than the one he's familiar with and it has thrown him. "There's no need to..." he says and I stop him with an upturned hand.

"Yes, there is, Steve. I do need to apologize to you; I want to apologize to you. It must have been very hurtful for you to... to have me cheat on you like that."

"That was years ago," he says nonchalantly, although I can see his eyes watering up, even if he isn't aware. "That's all water under the bridge."

I slide down to the floor to be closer to him and with heartfelt and apologetic eyes, I place my hands on his left knee. "When you met me first I was in an awful mess," I say, staring him in the eye, as if forcing him to listen. "I've never told this to a living soul but I was actually suicidal at the time. I was pregnant with Janice and I felt abandoned by my lover and my mother; my father had taken off years before... I felt very, very alone."

Steve wipes a tear from his left eye and I'm sure that he's hoping and praying that I'll stop talking... but I don't. "You saved my life, Steve. It can't have been much of a bargain for you and maybe you knew that it was a losing proposition for you to begin with, yet you still took the chance; you still opened your heart to me and took care of me, took care of us both. Before you came along, I was considering aborting Janice... so maybe you saved her life, as well. But you need to know, Steve. You need to know what you did, how much you meant to me, to Janice... you need to know how much I am indebted to you... for your kindness to us both..."

"Stop," he says, "please stop." Tears stream down his cheeks and his shoulders are shaking from his sobbing. He places a hand to his eyes as if to shield his crying; as if he doesn't want me to see him weep.

"It's okay," I say. "It's okay to cry, Steve. I lift myself up off the floor and sit beside him, placing both my arms around him and I hold him tenderly, almost as if he belonged to me; as if he was my father and my son and my brother...

"I'm so thankful you came into my life," I say softly. "You're such a brave and caring man and even though I know I've hurt you in the past... I'll always love you."

Steve turns his body to me and he hugs me tightly. His tears flow freely now as he holds the back of my head so that my face rests against his chest, his chin resting on the top of my head. "And I'll always love you, too," he says

119

softly. "I'd do it all over again in a heartbeat," he whispers, "and I wouldn't think twice."

Unable to contain my own tears, we both hold each other tightly... and weep. I'm not sure why I'm weeping. I don't know if I'm crying for Steve or crying for myself or crying for poor Janice, who must have been dealt a raw deal in the sad and sorry story of my life so far.

Perhaps I'm crying for all of us and I'm wondering how three caring and loving people— people who obviously care and have love for one another—can be so disconnected and seem distant from each other that we act like we don't care; or maybe we act like we don't care to avoid scenes like this.

Perhaps if we all stopped acting like we don't have a care in the world and ceased hiding our true thoughts and feelings for one another... then perhaps all we would do is cry.

Instead of meeting for lunch and talking about our superficial lives, what if, instead, we met and truly opened up to one another? Maybe Dr. Roberts would ask, 'What is the hidden fear inside of us that would prevent that?' Perhaps our deepest fear is that we'd fall helplessly into each other's arms and we'd cry and we'd cry and we wouldn't be able to stop.

CHAPTER 11

Martin waits for me outside his apartment and as soon as I see his kind and happy face, I smile. I double park and quickly run out to greet him with a kiss and a hug. I can see an instant look of desire and approval in his eyes, which I find really sexy. When I disengage from our embrace, his body seems disappointed, as if the hug was too brief. It makes me feel hopeful that we may have a healthy sex life, after all.

We throw his duffel bag into the trunk and without any further delay, I pull out into moderate traffic. I'm delighted to be leaving the city and so looking forward to our weekend getaway. I'm in a buoyant mood, as my choice of *Beach Boys* music testifies. Perhaps my mood is infectious as Martin looks equally happy; a broad smile on his face as his head bobs to the music.

I genuinely feel like I'm entering a new phase of my life; as if something in me has shifted and I'm ready to end my aloneness and put myself out there more. I don't just mean in terms of romantic relationships; just life, in general. Am I less afraid, perhaps? Have I conquered some hidden fears that were keeping me isolated and alone? When I think of what those fears might have been, I have to admit that I'm not really sure.

Whatever has happened to me in the past week or two has been instrumental in the shift and perhaps it's a combination of things, rather than one singular event or circumstance. I think that it's safe to say that it all started with meeting Martin that evening at the restaurant.

Up to that point, I had been stuck in my usual

routine and yet the spontaneity of the evening seemed to pull me right out of myself and my world. In the company of Martin, I got to be someone else for a change; maybe I got to be the old me that I had put away a long time ago. I got to reengage with the old me that was fun and carefree and sexy and had a positive, optimistic view on life.

Since meeting Martin, even my therapy sessions have taken on a deeper significance and meaning. I'm no longer talking and thinking about Bill and maybe having someone new in my world has been just the impetus I need to be able to finally say goodbye to that phase of my life? Dr. Roberts always referred to it as my grief stage but even I could see that I was wallowing for way too long in grief and after a while was even boring myself with my incessant self-exploration (which to others, like Janice, probably, looked more like self-pity).

My lunch the other day with Steve was mind blowing. The person I was up until meeting Martin would not have been so bold to have related to Steve in that deep, authentic and vulnerable way. Imagine if I was so bold in all my relationships? Whoever said 'let bygones be bygones' obviously never apologized to anyone in their lives. If they did, they would have seen how powerful an apology can be. I'm now going to apologize to everyone I know; even those that I think should be apologizing to me.

Reading the *Zen and the Art of Relationship* book from cover to cover has also really helped and has given me a brand new attitude to how precious being present in the moment is. It would stand to reason that if we could get the present moment right, there would be no need for future apologies. I'm going to be much more courageous with my present moments from now on. I'm not going to let things that bother me pass me by without challenging the person first.

If someone says something that I don't think is true, I'm going to call them on it. If someone says something that hurts me in some way, I'm not going to suck it up like I used to; I'm going to say something. I'm going to honor my feelings in the moment and not brush them under the proverbial carpet like I have been doing. Not wanting to 'rock the boat' or 'cause a scene' before didn't make it any easier to have a successful future with that person; in fact, quite the opposite. Things unsaid have a habit of festering in people's minds and when enough of them group together, they can grow into formidable resentments that are rarely dealt with in the future.

Things unsaid between Bill and I built up into such ferocious resentments—on both our parts, I'm sure—that instead of dealing with them, we grew apart. Over the years, we grew apart so much that we didn't even have the energy, will or motivation to fix what might be wrong in our relationship. As far as he was concerned we just 'grew out of love' and 'moving on' was the answer for us both. What a fool I was to agree and not fight.

I agreed with him that things were 'too far gone' and we had grown apart to the point of being two different people than the ones that had fallen in love with each other. Maybe it was easier to split than it was to explore the past. Why would it have been any easier to say the things to each other that we didn't have the courage to say in all those present moments that we let slip away?

I'm never going to make the same mistakes again. Even if Martin and I have no real future together, I'm going to challenge every moment of our togetherness and I don't care if he perceives me as some nagging, neurotic pain in the ass. I care about my well-being and my future happiness. I do want to be happy and I do want all my relationships to be healthy and happy.

As Dr. Roberts would say, 'What you want is not going to happen all by itself; you have to be brave to take the actions to get the results that you desire.' Amen, sister.

"What do you look for in a relationship?" I ask Martin as I set the cruise control, now that the traffic on the five freeway has thinned out.

"Honesty, loyalty and integrity are top of my list," Martin answers and by the way he answers I can tell that he hasn't given it much thought. It's probably not the kind of conversation a guy wants to have as we drive up north for a mini vacation but it's the only kind of conversation that I want to have and talking about the music we like or the movies we've seen isn't going to cut it for me anymore: forget the sizzle, I want steak.

As I persist with my questioning, in fairness to Martin, he does relax more into it and the conversation becomes more of a natural give and take. He does seem curious enough to listen to my theories and he even asks some really good questions.

Guys get a bad rap for not wanting to talk about their feelings but maybe women are in part to blame for that. One thing that I learned from working with people where English was not their first language was this: just because they don't speak your language doesn't mean that they're dumb. Maybe we just need to talk more slowly, use simpler words and have lots more patience.

Even though it took us over eight hours to get to Doris and Chuck's place, I was still feeling energized. I talked Martin's ear off the whole way and I think I just broke a record for the length of time a woman can talk to a guy about relationships and not have the guy change the subject or express a desire to strangle her. Martin continued to ask good questions and he didn't stop smiling the whole time. I think he's a keeper.

Doris and Chuck look tired from the week's exhaustions and Doris quickly shows us where to put our things. She has been cooking for a while and I know that she loves to have a glass of wine or two while she cooks and judging by her state of inebriation, it looks like tonight is no exception. Martin fits right in and doesn't at all seem socially awkward around them as we sit down to Doris' lovely meal. There's so much food, I at first wondered if she was expecting more people but as the evening wears on, no one else shows up and the moment for asking passes.

As we talk about how everyone met and relationships in general, I get the impression that things are not going well between them. It's not like they were arguing or passing snide comments about each other; it just seems like there is a distance between them that suggests they are having problems. Being married is tough and my heart goes out to them. I hope I can get a chance to talk to Doris alone sometime before all her guests begin arriving.

Doris shows us to one of the guest bedrooms upstairs and I get a cold shiver up my spine when I see that there's only one bed. She explains that we need to move downstairs the following evening and crash on the floor in the office so as to give the bed to our mom, if she decides to stay over. When Doris finally leaves and closes the door, Martin and I stand awkwardly looking at each other; perhaps each of us wondering, what now?

I'm feeling more terrified than sexy and I know that if we have a repeat of our first evening in the bedroom, there will be no going back: end of relationship. I realize that for us to have any chance of a future together, I need to take charge. Taking a few deep breaths, I calm myself. Standing before him, I strain my memory to remember the chapter in the Zen book that deals with physical intimacy.

"Take off your clothes," I say, hoping to sound

commanding but also soft and sexy. Not sure if I attained all that as he looks at me with terrified eyes. "Are you nervous?" I ask.

"Nervous about what?" he asks me back.

"I thought we were going to try honest communication?" I say.

"I'm a little bit nervous, sure," he then admits. "The last time wasn't great."

His admission of the fact that he is nervous and scared to have a repeat of our previous disaster seems to relax us both; we each smile at the same time, albeit nervously.

"Would it help if I took off my clothes first?" I ask and although he remains silent, I can tell from the instant relaxation of his body that he thinks it a very good idea, yes.

I undress slowly and deliberately and try to maintain eye contact with him the whole time. It only gets awkward and weird when I have to bend down to release the straps on my shoes; as I look up at him, I feel like my neck is going to snap. He doesn't say anything this whole time but I can tell by the dilation of his pupils that he likes what he sees.

The desire he must be feeling in his body is almost palpable and gives me confirmation that I'm going about this the right way. I'd hate to think that he was just standing there, feeling apathetic or worse... hating how my body looks. I now thank myself for being disciplined enough to force my body to do yoga most mornings.

I don't have the nerve to completely undress so for the moment, I leave my undies on and putting my hands by sides, I hope to signal him to begin his own undressing. I can tell that this experience is so new for him that he's unsure how to go about it (Shirt first? Pants first? Shoes and socks?). Perhaps he's also wondering to himself if it's okay for him to talk.

Thankfully he doesn't. I already told him on the drive up that when he is feeling nervous, he has a tendency to make a joke. I'm self-conscious enough as it is and I don't think I could take him joking about anything concerning my body, right now, thank you very much.

I'm also thankful that the lights are dimmed and I don't dare look at my own exposed skin for fear of finding wrinkles, creases, blotches, sun tan lines and all sorts of areas I most likely would freak out about if I was sober and looking at them in the cold harsh lights of my bathroom.

When he strips down to his boxers, I bite the bullet and very slowly slip my underwear off and let them fall down my legs to the floor. He's a perfect gentleman as his eyes remain focused on my eyes and he gives me the respect of not shifting his gaze to leer lustfully at my female parts.

"Now you can't lie," I say to him as he removes his boxers and drops them to the floor. "A naked person can't tell lies."

"When was the last time you had sex?" he asks with a smirk. There's no way I'm going to answer that and so I step closer to him so that our bodies are almost touching. I don't look but I can feel him getting aroused and his arousal makes my body tingle with excitement. His eyes keep looking from my eyes to my lips and back again and as he leans in to kiss me, I stop his lips with my fingers.

As much as I want our lips to meet, I want this exercise to work and I'm prepared to risk losing our sexy mood if it means finding out right here and now if our bodies are sexually compatible or not. "What do you say we let our bodies get to know each other, first?" I ask silently.

He very tenderly agrees with his smiling eyes and I love him for it. I don't know how many men would have either insisted that we 'get it on' at this point or would have already walked out in frustration or annoyance. Martin's eyes are still smiling at me and if his continued arousal is anything to go by, he hasn't lost interest in the slightest.

I take his right arm in my left hand and with my right hand, I very gently stroke his skin with my fingers. From the look on his face, I can tell that he likes it; it feels to me like his body just shivered as a tingling sensation surfed through his body. As my fingers, very gently, continue to stroke the skin of his shoulders and chest, he smiles and his face seems to transform into the relaxed pose of someone who is getting a very pleasurable massage.

I can tell from the look in his eyes that he is wondering if he should be doing something for me, so I take his right hand in both my hands and pull it slowly towards my left arm. "Put your mind into the tips of your fingers and touch everything except the obvious," I tell him.

His touch is so light and gentle that it surprises me. I'm not used to being touched by a man in such a tender way. My body yields to his touch and suddenly I'm the one with the pleasurable look on my face; my flesh tingling with pleasure and arousal. Even though we're obviously grown adults, as we look into each other's eyes, I feel like we're just a pair of two playful kids, playing a secret game that's not just fun but daring.

Even though I'm stripped bare, my body feels warm and energized; yet weirdly, it feels relaxed at the same time. Even as we continue to gently stroke each other's bodies in a non-sexual way, I still can't help but feel aroused. I know that he's feeling the same as I can hear his breathing get deeper and he's practically moaning on the deep exhales.

"Frances," he says softly.

"Yes?" I answer quietly as I rub my nose gently against his, our lips almost touching.

"Are we going to have sex soon?" he asks.

Even though our bodies are, no doubt, both primed for the most luscious love-making ever, I want to continue feeling the thrill of this Zen touch or whatever it is for a bit longer. My body has so been starved of touch and it's been such a long time of depravity, it's like it needs to catch up and make up for lost time.

When I feel like I can't put off Martin's ardor any longer, I take him by the hand and lead him slowly towards the bed. In tandem with our slow and soft caresses, as our lips gently meet, waves of pleasure pulse through my body from my lips and my skin to my head and to my toes. I hear myself groan as he lifts my body and gently lowers me down onto the bed.

I heave his body tight into my mine. With the fingers of my right hand, I caress his hair. His masculine excitement is intoxicating and as my fingers stroke his hair, I get the urge to grab hold of a fistful and I pull the hair at the back of his head as hard as I can. He doesn't wince and I can feel him get emboldened by my surprising act of playful aggression.

As I pull harder, I can feel him get more manly and assertive; more primal, almost. Our kissing gets more intense and his lips meet mine with such intensity I have to pull back or it will hurt. I want our foreplay to last longer but already he's inside me and as soon as he enters I get a feeling of panic surprise me from I don't know where; as if I'm being ambushed by a saboteur emotion that has come to ruin the party.

And ruin it, it does. My body feels an instant jolt of panic and then it goes numb; all sensation in my entire body, from head to toe, switches off like an electrical shutdown. As I experience my own private rolling blackout, I notice that my eyes have opened wider and I probably have a look of terror on my face.

Oblivious to my meltdown, Martin continues to exist in his own pleasure house of fun and lust. Perhaps he's confusing my look of terror for one of ecstasy and he almost shouts out with cries of joy when he comes. I hold him as he collapses his body beside me. He's taking deep breaths and perspiring profusely as if he just ran a marathon.

As he experiences a bodily shutdown of his own, I wonder to myself about what has just happened. What is it about Martin that had such a profound effect upon me? Is my body scared of him in some way; as if warning me that this is not right? By not being sensitive to me, did he rush things and in so doing break our connection, scaring me?

Once again, even though I'm lying in post-coital intimacy with a man, I'm nevertheless feeling alienated and alone. As Martin snuggles his face into my neck and wraps one of his sweaty legs over one of my own, I'm left wondering if maybe our sexual incompatibility is not something that actually can be fixed, after all.

CHAPTER 12

Even though I slept soundly, I wake up feeling a bit on the grumpy side. I'm awake but I'm having a hard time opening my eyes. Judging from the indentation of Martin's elbow on the pillow beside me, it can only mean that he is propped up and wide awake, waiting for me to wake up. Sure enough, when I do finally open my eyes, Martin, looking like a puppy, seems ready and eager to start our day.

While I stall, dreading actually moving my body and getting my ass out of bed, I make small talk. I ask him what he has been thinking since he's been sitting up waiting, presumably staring into space. He tells me that he's been watching me sleep and that I look beautiful. It's very sweet of him to say so but let's face it: no one looks beautiful first thing in the morning.

"That's very sweet," I say, still not opening my eyes. "What were you *really* thinking?"

I don't have to look at him to know that there's something on his mind and I brace myself when he tells me that he's now going to practice honest communication. By his tone, I know that what he is going to tell me isn't going to be the cheerful good news that I expected my day to be starting off with.

"I was just wondering about the future and, uh... checking out the wrinkles around your eyes and stuff," he says calmly. Seriously? This is what he wants to talk about first thing in the morning after another miserable night of sexual miscommunication?

"Do I look old and haggard in the morning, sweetheart?" I say sarcastically and right away, I'm regretting saying it the way I did. Jeez, I can be such a bitch, sometimes.

"No, not at all," he says and if he has any sense, he should stop right there. He doesn't. "Maybe down the road you will, I guess. I don't know," he says and I feel like dumping his sorry ass, right here and now.

Instead of saying what I really want to say, however, like, "You've got to be kidding me with this shit!" or something along those lines, I figure that I should give the guy credit for trying something new. What kind of a hypocrite would I be if I talked about the need for honest communication and then shot him down when he had actually listened to what I said, took it to heart and then practiced it? If I wasn't feeling so miserable, I guess I should be giving the guy a slap on the back or a high five or something.

I manage to put a smile on my face and pretty much quote to him what any self-respecting self-help book on conscious relationship would recommend as a response. "Everybody ages," I tell him, although I almost throw up in my mouth when I say the words.

"I'm just surprised that it's not a touchy subject for you, being a woman and all, given how society is about aging," he says and, when he doesn't have the sense to shut up about it, I can't restrain myself any longer and I pretty much lose it.

"Yeah, well, I'd be lying to you if I said that I was okay with aging and losing my looks. Are you kidding? It sucks rocks. What's the worst thing that can happen as a guy ages? He gets salt and pepper hair? Which for most guys is an improvement to their looks, they look more distinguished even. Or big deal, maybe a guy goes bald. Thanks to Bruce Willis and Vin Diesel, something that used to be considered geeky is now considered deadly sexy. So yeah, I'm majorly pissed off about the whole aging thing and the unfairness of it... how men can get away with aging while women get royally screwed!"

I can tell by the shocked look upon his face that this wasn't the kind of honest communication he was expecting and after a few seconds of looking like his head is scrambling for something redeeming to say, he looks at me and smiles. "What are our plans for breakfast?" he asks cheerfully and I almost say that that's the kind of question he should have started the day off with... but I don't.

"Breakfast?" I ask, like I'm completely thrown for a response, which I am. "I don't know."

"I really like this honest communication thing," he says, smiling.

"Yeah," I say and I have to work real hard not to give a catty response. "Yeah, it's really important," I finally manage to say, the mental image of Dr. Roberts' face bearing down on me in my mind. "Thank you for being honest with me," I say and give him a peck on the lips. "Let's go get breakfast."

As Martin puts his clothes on, I lock the bathroom door behind me and before I do anything else, I check out my face in the mirror. Apart from some minor shadows beneath my eyes, I don't look too bad. I look pretty good for a 38 year old woman with two marriages, especially one who gave birth two generations ago, that is. I grab my cosmetics bag and take a few products out of it.

I try to imagine what my face looks like to a 24 year old guy who's used to dating women just out of college. I tilt my head sideways to catch the best light which forces me to inspect my skin with eyes that are now so far to the extreme of my eye sockets that they hurt. I've got crow's feet and lines everywhere; not to mention that, on the side of my face that still has pillow marks, my skin looks so blotchy, that if Martin got real close, he just might mistake my face for an uncooked hamburger or something.

What a friggin' idiot. Instead of giving me compliments and assurances, he picks the one thing that totally sets us apart as the topic of our "honest" communication. When it comes to making a woman feel secure, why are guys such lamebrain dumbass mindless d-bags most of the time? I don't need this and I'd have to be out of my mind to sign up for a relationship that's going to make me so insecure about my looks. I'm sure I'll be considering cosmetic surgery as soon as I hit the big 4-0.

I put on some moisturizer and a light application of makeup and make a decision. For the rest of our time here, I won't bring up the subject. We'll have a pleasant weekend and, when I finally drop him back to his place, I'll tell him that it's not working out and that we should be friends or something. If I am going to date, I'm definitely going older. I want to be with someone mature who thinks that I'm desirable at any age. All the better if the guy is ten, twenty years older; he'll so think that he hit the jackpot, that I'll never have to worry about my looks, ever again.

When I finally leave the bathroom, Martin is sitting in a chair leafing through a book that I assume he found lying around. The volume obviously doesn't hold his interest, so I don't ask the title.

"You look fantastic," he says and instead of saying 'too little, too late,' which totally slides through my mind, I give him a polite smile of appreciation. I remind myself that allowing my inner bitch to come out and play may be fun in the short term but would most likely do more harm than good and that's not what I'm about anymore, anyway.

"Is everything okay?" he asks. Although he's referring to the amount of time I just spent in the bathroom, what I sense he's really asking is, 'Are we okay?'

"Yeah," I answer brightly. "Not used to eating so much food, I guess."

What I really want to say is, 'No, we're not okay and you may want to know that the reason I spent so long in the bathroom is not because I ate too much food but because getting my complexion to look vibrantly young, healthy and natural doesn't just take oodles of time but it requires a large measure of skill and artistry, not to mention a small fortune spent on expensive "age-defying" products, as well.'

I want to look him in the eye and ask him, 'Do you know how difficult it is to get the balance just right between applying so little makeup that it looks like I'm hardly wearing any at all and not so much makeup that looks like I just stepped out of Madame Tussauds wax museum? It's not just a skill, it's a friggin' science and I hate doing it just as much as you guys hate sitting around leafing through boring books or standing by the door rattling your car keys and asking, 'Are you ready, now?' every two friggin' seconds.'

When we walk down to the kitchen, Doris and Chuck are sitting at the kitchen table. They are both still wearing their house robes and slippers. I didn't hear any conversation as we approached, so it appears as if they are sitting silently together, a cup of coffee in each of their hands. I don't smell the aroma of food cooking and besides milk and sugar, there's no sign of food on the table before them. They both look so hung-over and/or depressed and disheveled that they look like they could easily have escaped the local psych ward.

"Morning all," I say as we enter and judging by their silent shudders of response, my greeting may have been too loud, bright and cheery for their sensibilities. "Did you two have breakfast, already?" I ask.

"Not yet. We were waiting for you guys," Doris

answers, barely lifting her head to greet us. "Wasn't sure what you guys wanted for breakfast, otherwise..." she says, not finishing her sentence.

"What do you have?" I ask as I pull the door open on her huge fridge and explore its packed-to-capacity contents.

"What don't I have?" Doris asks.

"Seriously," I say, feeling overwhelmed with choice. "Let me make breakfast," I suggest as Doris shifts in her chair, looking like she's finally winning the mental battle to move her body. "Everybody okay with eggs?" I ask.

"Sure," Doris says and both Chuck and Martin nod their heads.

"Can I help?" Martin asks and he looks so wide-eyed and keen that I believe that it must be a genuine offer. I don't know many guys from my past who sincerely wanted to help out in the kitchen and when I give him a smile of appreciation, his response grin makes me smile even wider.

"No, I'm good. You just relax," I say, which I'm now realizing was my rote response when Bill used to lamely ask the same question. Bill never really wanted to help so declining his offer was a way to let him off of the hook. When I answer the question this time, I surprise myself because I actually mean it. "Want some coffee?" I ask Martin.

"Yes, please," he answers.

"There's some made in the pot," Doris says unenthusiastically and when Martin just about sniggers, I almost join him.

"Great," he says, looking straight at me with a knowing smirk. I'm not sure what he finds funny but I'm guessing that it's the catatonic state of our hosts that's amusing him. Something about his impish grin and knowing look brings out the inner child in me and as if we're sharing a secret joke, we both avoid each other's direct gaze for fear of making each other burst out laughing.

As I take out a box of eggs from the fridge, I'm wondering to myself what I could make to cheer Doris up a little. I seem to remember that she liked to order *Eggs Benedict* when we were getting breakfast out, so I look to see if she has all the ingredients. Indeed she does. Martin sits at the table with his coffee and staring straight at me as if I was the most fascinating thing that he's ever seen, he doesn't even try to make conversation with the others.

Every time I steal a glance his way, I notice that his intense gaze on me hasn't shifted. His attention to me is exhilarating and every time our eyes meet, I can't seem to keep myself from smiling like a bashful teen.

Martin has a strange effect on me, one that I haven't, as yet, demystified. The warm and fuzzy feeling that I have in my chest right now is not how I woke up this morning and I know that I would not be feeling this way if Martin was not here. It reminds me of how I used to feel with Janice, when she was little. Some days I'd wake up like a grouchy old bear but, with one look at her innocent and tender face, I'd be instantaneously feeling all soft and squishy inside. Some days I didn't even know that I was in a bad mood until she smiled at me and I would instantly recognize that, up until that moment, I had been in a dark place.

What is it about other people in my life that bring out completely different moods in me? Unless they interfere with me in some way, most people don't affect me one way or another. I might look at someone and say, 'Oh, that person has an honest face,' or, 'That person has a sad face,' or whatever, but a few people I meet seem to have a much more profound effect.

Janice and Martin have a similar effect that when I

look at them, I feel warm inside and I want to embrace them and protect them from the harshness of the world. With Steve, I felt maybe competitive with him, almost as if I didn't fully trust him and had to keep a good eye on him, all of the time. When I saw Bill, I had an urge for him to embrace me and a desire to sink my face deep against his chest and have him hold me like he would never let me go.

The way that I feel about John the waiter is similar to the way that I used to feel about Jim Costas. The first time that I saw Jonathan, it was as if something primal inside of me got all stirred up and I wanted to rip off his clothes... actually, no, scratch that: I wanted him to rip off *my* clothes, manhandle me in the basest way imaginable by throwing me to his bed and having his way with me until we were both too sore to move any longer.

"How are those eggs coming along?" Martin asks and I can sense that his concern is not so much about the breakfast but rather that something inside him knew that he was losing me to my thoughts and he wants to pull me back.

"Almost there," I say as I take a deep breath to rejoin the not-so-pleasant here and now.

Nobody says much beyond small talk during breakfast but Doris appears to be coming back to full function as she greedily eats up the Eggs Benedict. "This is amazing," she says and everyone agrees. Martin plays footsies with me under the table, which really takes me back.

Back in our room, we pack our stuff up in order to relocate downstairs to the office. "Leave your bag at the door with mine," I tell Martin as I pull off the sheets of the bed. "I'll bring them both down later."

"What can I help you with, Frances?" Martin asks.

"That's really nice of you, sweetie, but I thought

that you'd like to go explore the town while Doris and I set up for the evening. Did you bring a camera?"

"Of course," he says, "always."

"Go be a tourist for the day. It will give me a chance to hang out with my sister. I don't get the opportunity very often. Do you mind?"

"No, that's fine. I understand. It's a beautiful day."

"Go explore," I say and give him a quick kiss good-bye. "See you later at the party."

When Martin heads off, I help Doris in the kitchen. "I think it's really nice of you to bake mom a cake rather than buy one in the store," I tell her as she mixes together the ingredients. "Much more personal and caring."

"Yeah, I think so," Doris agrees.

When Doris puts the cake into the oven, she sends Chuck off to the store to pick up all of the stuff that she has on order: party platters of food, alcohol, chips and so on. "Want a beer?" she asks as she takes two Mexican beers from the fridge. I don't like Mexican beer but I want to bond with my sister, so I take what she's offering. "Let's sit outside," she says, grabbing her cigarettes.

Sitting out back, I take in the beautiful view of the distant mountains and the sheer mass of green foliage growing everywhere; it acts as a balm to my LA desert-accustomed eyes.

"Do you miss it?" she asks, noticing my appreciation as I sweep the panorama with my eyes.

"I miss the green," I say, "and the clean air, of course."

"I could never live down there. Why don't you move back up?"

"I don't know," I say, not even considering it. "I'm happy."

"You're happy?" she scoffs, as if my choice of word

offends her. "How can anyone be happy in LA?"

"Are you happy up here?" I ask.

"Happier than I'd be down there," she says. "I don't know anyone that's genuinely happy," she then says, after a pause. "Do you?"

"Not happy all of the time, no."

"So, how's tricks?" she asks, as if we have both run out of conversation already. I don't want to have the usual superficial connection with my sister but I'm not sure how to begin to have a more deeply meaningful one. Even though Doris is a couple of years younger than I, she has always acted as if she were the older one. If I was being honest, I'd admit to being intimidated by her. She can be very gruff and dismissive of me and as a consequence, I don't enjoy talking with her very much.

"I'm sorry," I say.

"You're sorry for what?" she asks.

"I'm sorry for being a lousy sister. I'm your big sister and I don't think I've ever, I don't know, looked after you like a big sister should. And I'm sorry."

Doris puts her beer down and turns her body towards me. She looks at me hard, as if to get a better read of my face and body language. "You're sorry for not being a big sister?" she asks, as if seeking greater clarification.

"You were the little sister," I say, probing my thoughts for the right things to say. "You should have gotten more attention than you did but it's like that I got all the attention and you were... you got short-changed."

Doris looks at me with a concerned look on her face, as if I'm taking her in a direction she isn't at all comfortable with. "You mean you got more attention because you were the pretty one?" she asks. "I'm over that," she then says quickly. "That shit stopped hurting in high school."

"Even still," I say. "I'm sorry."

"What the hell have you got to be sorry about, exactly?" she asks angrily. "It's not like you were doing something on purpose, was it? It's not your fault that people thought you were the good-looking sister. That's the shit all young girls have to put up with, the 'Oh, you're so pretty,' bullshit. You got lucky. I didn't. I don't see where you're to blame for that. Do you?"

"I could have been more… thoughtful," I say. "I could have tried to understand and to be more… compassionate towards you, include you more."

"Frances, seriously," Doris says and stops, as if she's thinking better of saying what she was going to say.

"What?"

"Nothing."

"What were you going to say?"

"You're just so… full of shit sometimes, that's all."

"Oh," I say, wondering what she means, as I go over what I've just been saying in my head. "In what way?"

"Every time you come up here, it's like we have to listen to your touchy-feely LA bullshit."

"You mean all my talk about Zen and honest communication and stuff?" I ask, referring to our dinner conversation of the previous evening.

"I didn't want to say anything in front of Martin but you can come across like some agony aunt advice columnist know-it-all sometimes. Your act just gets tired after a while."

"My 'act'"?

"You say stuff like it's true but people that know you know that it's a crock."

"What?" I ask, genuinely perplexed. What is she talking about?

"Never mind," Doris says, stamping out her

141

cigarette but on the ground. "I don't want to get into it."

"I want to know what you mean? What do I say that's a crock?" I insist.

"You talk about Jim Costas like he got you pregnant and then did a runner, for instance."

"Yeah?"

"Frances, you were sleeping with so many guys, how could the guy know for sure that he was the one that got you pregnant? You guys weren't even exclusive, for crying out loud. The guy was crazy about you. You were the one that kept him at a distance... but the way you tell it now, he broke your heart and abandoned you when you were in need. Now, that's not true at all, is it? Admit it."

"I don't say that he abandoned me..." I say, wondering how she seems to know so much about Jim Costas and what my life was like back then.

"That's what you make it sound like... look, forget about..."

"No, this is good," I say, glad that we're clearing the air. "What else? What other crock do I annoy you with?"

"I'm not trying to hurt you, Frances. We're family. If we don't call you on your shit, who will, right?"

"I agree. What else do I annoy you with?"

"You tell everyone that you've been married for fourteen years, which is true, but you conveniently forget to mention that you were separated for like five of those years," Doris says in a way that suggests that she has been waiting a long time to say these things to me. "Look, forget it... I'm not trying to get on your case, we all have shit we'd prefer not to mention. We all wish some stuff in our past happened differently that we spin a little in conversations with others."

"We were separated but we were still trying to work things out," I say. "I *was* married fourteen years up till

I actually signed the divorce."

"Yeah, I know." Doris says, as if she regrets having said anything at all. "I'm going to go check on the cake."

As Doris goes back into the kitchen I chide myself for my botched communication. Instead of getting closer to my sister, I'm making her angry and pushing her away even further. I've never seen her get so angry for no reason before. She seems to be in a lot of personal pain and I'm trying not to take what she says personally. How do I get her to open up and confide in me? Do I really come across like a New Age know-it-all?

I sit and wait and after about ten minutes, it occurs to me that she's not coming back any time soon. She took her beer with her, which is not a promising sign.

"What can I help you with?" I ask Doris as I rejoin her in the kitchen. I ask in such a way that I hope to indicate that this is a new me and if we can both forget the conversation out back, that would be terrific. To further make my point, I clasp my hands and rub them together in expectation of a new set of tasks.

"You want to mix a salad?" she asks. "There's three large bowls on the counter and take everything you need from the fridge."

"Will do," I say and I catch myself just in time from making a one finger salute.

When Chuck comes back from the store, we both help him unload. Doris sends him back off again and it wasn't clear to me what his mission was. I overheard 'pick them up' and 'store' so maybe he was to pick up some of mom's party guests while also going to a different store.

"I need a smoke," Doris says, when we finish unpacking all the store-bought goodies. I'm not sure if she said it to invite me to join her or if it was just an FYI. I pluck up my courage to follow her and take two Mexican beers with me. Once back outside, I hand her one as casually as I can, without comment.

"I was almost going to be in LA next weekend," she says as she exhales a plume of smoke.

"For work?" I ask.

"No, would you believe a relationship seminar?" she says. "I thought of you when I was signing up. It's more like something you'd be going to. You can have my tickets, if you like."

"You mean... like a couple's weekend retreat?"

"I guess," she answers. "I thought it might do us some good."

"You're not going?"

"The stuff we need to fix... I don't think a weekend in LA is going to do the trick."

"It could be a start, though, right?"

"Maybe," Doris says and as she exhales she looks off into the distance.

Feeling really excited about Doris sharing like this and not wanting to sound touchy-feely, I chose my words very carefully. "You don't want to work on your marriage?" I ask.

"I don't have a problem doing the work," Doris answers and turns to look at me. "But if I'm with the wrong partner... I just don't see the point."

"I see," I say, stunned by her admission.

"I'm not thinking of getting a divorce, if that's your next question," she says. "I just have to learn to live with my disappointment, that's all."

"I thought you two were..."

"What?"

"Good together?"

"We are good together," Doris says and either she's not being clear or I'm very confused about what she's

144

saying. "I just didn't think that things were going to get stale, so quick. We've only been married three years, for chrissakes."

"I understand," I say. "It got like that with me and Bill."

"What did?" she asks.

"The first few years were total bliss but as soon as a routine start settling in... he began to lose interest. Three years into marriage and I had to compete with his laptop for attention. I know how hurtful that can be."

"It's not like that," Doris says, dismissively. "Chuck never lost interest. Nothing has changed with him; he's crazy about me; probably crazier about me now than he was, even then."

"So..."

"So, it must be me, right? I don't find him attractive anymore. We get on great but he's more like a brother to me than a... husband. I won't let him touch me. The thought of being with him like that... sickens me."

"Wow," I say, lost for words or understanding. "I had no idea."

"How would you have any idea? It's not like I post this shit on FaceBook as an update." When my sister suddenly laughs at her own comment, I thankfully join in.

"Look," she says. "I went in with my eyes open, no regrets. I was ready to settle down; he was ready to settle down. Our interests were matched up on a matchmaking site. He checked all the boxes. At the time, I thought it was a match made in heaven."

"Let me ask you something," I say, feeling desperately like I want to give my sister some help or words of wisdom or say something that might guide her towards some epiphany or greater understanding. "When you met Chuck first... what was your primary feeling towards him?

How did he make you feel?"

"Terrific! He made me feel terrific. But that was all unreal, wasn't it? We were dating. We went to lovely restaurants; went on romantic dates to the movies and weekend getaways and stuff. Who doesn't feel terrific, having a blast going to romantic places all the time?"

"Don't get me started on romance," I say.

"So we get married. I didn't know the terrific feeling was going to go away so quick; I thought like in thirty years or something. Didn't know it could go away in an instant... like, the first time I shared a bathroom with him? Words to the wise? Get separate bathrooms... and never, ever offer to do your husband's laundry. The first time I saw the state of his underwear? Forget about it. A little bit of mystique in a relationship goes a long way, know what I mean?"

"Totally," I say.

"Don't get all worried about me, sis," she says looking at my face and I positively light up when she uses the word, 'sis.' "I'm well aware that this could just be a phase and that all of these feelings that I have could all go away tomorrow. Like I say, it's not like I'm planning on having an affair or getting a divorce or something."

"Glad to hear it," I say and I almost call her sis back.

"What was the point you were making? I think I cut you off."

"Oh, well, actually I was going to make a few points," I say, feeling like finally we're really bonding as true sisters should. "I know what you mean about the whole brother thing, trust me. With Bill and me, it was like we became roommates after a while and he wasn't too happy when I told him that, either, by the by."

"I can imagine," Doris says, taking another swig of beer.

"I was just wondering about how Chuck made you

146

feel, I mean, aside from the matching up and the dating and everything..."

"How he made me feel?" Doris asks, not understanding.

"I was thinking about this very thing, just what we're talking about, earlier today, as a matter of fact..." I say and as I tell her about how each of the men in my life made me feel, I can see her thinking hard, like she was really listening to me.

"Who's John the waiter?" she asks.

"Just some guy. We went on a date, sort of, and I'll never see him again but I mention him as an example..."

"Why would you never see him again?" she asks.

"Because he's a player and he's manipulative and..."

"But he sounds like, out of all of your men, that he's the best... choice. Don't you think?" she asks and I look at her with obvious puzzlement on my face. "Here's what you just told me," she says, looking like she's getting her thoughts in order. "I'm not even going to include Steve here because, aside from you and mom, no one takes the guy seriously."

"Okay," I say weakly but I want her to continue, so I don't say anything else.

"Bill makes you feel like you want him to put his arm around you and protect you, take care of you and stuff... which, to me, sounds like you see him like a father, right?"

"Okay."

"Just like your daughter, Janice, you want to put *your* arm around Martin and protect him... which sounds like you see him as maybe a son?"

"Okay," I say and all of a sudden I'm feeling nauseous.

"John the waiter you want to make children with...

147

you see him as a lover, which, as I say, is the most appropriate kind of relationship for you, right?"

For someone who has never been in therapy, who abhors self-help books, sometimes I feel like my sister has so much intuition and common sense that she constantly hits them out of the park. I don't know how to answer her and all I can think about is: what if she's right?

"Hey, don't listen to me," she then says, as if my facial expression is troubling her. "I'm the one in marriage poop, what the heck do I know?"

When I smile, I can see that it makes her feel better and she slaps my knee with her hand. "Let's go make some icing for the cake, huh?" she says and stands.

CHAPTER 13

Time moves much quicker after the little chat with my sister. Guests begin arriving and need looking after; some of the foods need to be cooked; the beer needs to be kept cold and Chuck is sent for a few more bags of ice and other incidentals. I don't have time to think about much but, as I cook and prepare food and greet people that I barely know, I begin to miss the comforting and happy face of Martin. I begin to miss how he makes me feel inside.

It's strange being with my sister; it's like we know each other so well but at the same time it feels like we don't know each other at all. I'm not even sure that we like each other. I certainly get a feeling from her sometimes that she doesn't like me or, at the very least, I seem to get on her nerves. I feel like sometimes she'd like to slap me across the face and say something like, 'snap out of it,' or maybe, 'grow the fuck up,' or something similar.

When our mom arrives, I can immediately see their strong bond. It's like they really like each other. Like my sis, mom also has a tendency to treat me like I'm some kind of annoyance; a family fuck-up that they have to put up with. Would we all hang out together if we weren't blood related? No.

Perhaps I'm being too hard on them. I left home at seventeen to go to college in LA. I've really only been back for short visits here and there and that's mainly been for occasions where I felt obliged to return: Thanksgivings, major birthdays, weddings of mutual friends or relatives, and so on. I can't expect them to be overly friendly to me when I've hardly made much effort to spend time up here and get to know them as the adult I've become. How could I expect them to know me beyond what they remember of me when I was a kid?

Do they resent me for spending so much time away? Do they resent me for leaving to live, not just miles away but relocating to LA of all places; somewhere that most Northern Californian's consider the smelly armpit of the Golden State? As I look around at my mom and my sis and the early visiting guests, I notice how familiar and comfortable they all are with each other; how close-knit they are as a group. There's a much greater sense of community up here than the vast social wasteland of Los Angeles where most people, including myself, don't even know our own neighbors.

"How are you doing, sweetie?" my mom finally acknowledges me, having pulled herself away from her fawning friends. I can almost sense her reluctance to leave the warmth of her group and come greet me as I unwrap a sandwich platter at the kitchen table. She doesn't hug me but instead places her hand on my right shoulder.

"I'm doing great, momma," I say as I turn to give her a proper hug.

"Did Janny not come?" she asks.

"She'll be here later. She's getting a ride with Steve," I answer. At what point in their relationship did my mom start calling Janice, "Janny" and how often do they talk to each other, anyway, I wonder?

"She didn't come with you?"

"No. She had stuff to do and wanted to leave later in the day. She has all these deadlines with school and everything," I say, not wanting to explain the real reason she didn't ride with me.

"Yeah, she seems to love it there," my mom says; her affection for my daughter evident in the way that she speaks about her. "I hope she gets something out of it, afterwards."

"You mean like a career? I know, right?"

"Throw a stone and you'll hit a filmmaker in LA. It's getting to be that way up here, as well," she says, a tone of derision in her voice.

"I think she'll do okay. She's a very talented young woman," I say, not fully believing it. I have absolutely no way of knowing if my daughter has any filmmaking talent whatsoever.

"Is she coming alone?" my mom asks, looking at me closer, "or is she bringing a friend?"

I've no idea what my mom knows or doesn't know about Janice's choice of 'friend' these days but there's no way I'm having that kind of discussion with my mother. Although she has always been supportive of Janice, I doubt that she would approve of her present lifestyle in the city of freaks and I'm under no illusions that in my mom's head, whatever Janice does or doesn't do, I'm ultimately responsible for my daughter's choices.

"I think she said that she's coming alone," I answer breezily, secretly praying for a change of topic. "She said that she can't wait to see you."

"And what about you?" she asks, still not shifting her intense gaze. "I hear that you brought a friend?"

"Yes," I say, brightly, "I brought a nice young man with me, Martin."

"A *boy* friend?" she asks, putting an emphasis on the 'boy' part. Or is that my imagination?

"At this point, we're just friends," I answer, not shifting my eyes but rolling up the plastic wrap from the sandwich, hoping to signal that I need to get back to work real soon.

"But you are sleeping together," my mom says, like

it was a statement rather than a question. "You slept in the guest room last night?"

"Yes," I answer, thankful that it was a two part question.

"He's younger, I hear," she says, as if it's an accusation... or is that my imagination, also? Please god let this interrogation be over soon.

"There is an age difference," I admit. "It must be my thing. There was an age difference with both my ex-husbands. Steve is like..."

"Yeah, but they're men. It's more natural for the man to be older," my mom says and because she doesn't follow it up with anything else, I'm left to ponder her meaning.

"It is," I agree. "More socially acceptable, I guess." My mom doesn't say anything and I'm not sure what else she wants from me. "For the guy to be older," I continue, as if I'm implying that I'm assuming that her silence is an indication that she is waiting for me to finish my thought.

"As long as two people get along together," she says without much conviction.

There's always so much subtext going on with my mom whenever we talk that I have no idea what's going on in her skull when we do get together. It could be my imagination but it feels like she's judging me all the time; in fact, it feels like her mind has been made up a long time ago and she has since considered me to be nothing short of a royal fuck-up.

I feel like reminding her that she's not exactly the prize-winning relationship queen that she makes herself out to be; her second husband — my father — abandoned her to her fate and decided to make a family with a different woman in a different state. She barely mentions her first marriage except to state it merely as a historical fact.

"Relationships are tough," I say, knowing with full certainty that she could not deny my statement. I feel like saying that if she 'threw a stone' and hit someone in this very room that we're standing in, we'd find that every single person, young or old, is now or has, at some time in their past, experienced some difficulty in their relationship.

I wonder if she cross-examines Doris so intensely, as far as her marriage is concerned? I could think of a few questions for her to ask, like, 'Are you two sleeping together?' or 'Why aren't you giving me grand children?' or 'What's all this I hear about you two being sick to death of each other already, after just three years of marriage?'

"I'm sorry, mama," I blurt out.

"Sorry for what, sweetie?"

"I must be... such a disappointment to you. I left home when I was too young and all I seemed to do since was get into trouble after trouble. I must have been a constant worry to you and at this stage of my life, I'm still not settled and happy."

My mom looks searchingly at me for what seems like a long time. I've no idea what she's thinking but only her eyes are moving, her body fixed in place. "You're not happy, sweet pea?" she asks in a voice that overflows with pity and misplaced commiseration. This is what she took from my apology?

"No, I *am* happy..." I say, wondering if I should couch the apology in different terms.

"But you just said that you weren't happy?"

"No, I'm happy, I mean, not happy all-the-time-happy, I mean, who is, right?" I blabber and I know in my heart that I've just blundered my chance at a deeper mother-daughter connection. Not only am I a screw-up in her eyes but I've just admitted to her that I'm a desperately unhappy screw-up. That's how she's going to look at me

153

from now on; there's no easy, immediate way to recover from this.

"What I'm trying to say is that I'm sure you must see me as a screw-up, an unhappy screw-up, and I was apologizing for seeming that way to you and, for that, I'm sorry..."

My mom looks at me like she might need to call the nice men in the white coats. With the way I'm going about this, not being able to find the right words to communicate with her, I don't blame her.

"Martin's here," Doris says to me as she walks in from the front room.

"Oh, I need to see him," I say and my absolute relief must be blatant as heck when I break away from my mom. As I'm going, I could swear that my mom shared a private look with Doris as if to say, 'Yeah, you were right: she is a basket case with more than a few screws loose,' or something similar.

"Hi, sweetie. Have a nice walk?" I greet Martin with a kiss and a smile. I'm so glad to see him that I feel like taking him by the hand, getting back into the car and driving us both back to LA right away.

"Can I help with something?" he asks and I almost swoon at his eagerness to make me happy. As I sit him down in a nice armchair in the front room, I'm wondering why I don't really want to introduce him to my mom, just yet. Perhaps my discussion with her is still too raw in my memory and although I'm sure she will be nice to Martin, I'm also pretty sure that she will judge him. I want to protect him from that.

Even though our sex isn't great, I feel like it is getting better and I do love our closeness and the intimacy that we both seem to crave together. I'm actually looking forward to being alone and naked with him and the thought of having that in a few hours gives me the courage to go through with the rest of the evening. I go to my purse and take out the book about Tantric Sex that I brought with me. "This will blow your mind," I whisper to him as I surreptitiously hand him the book, looking around to make sure no one is looking.

To be honest, the book is really boring, which is one reason that I never got past the first few pages. I want our sex to get better, however, so I desperately want him to read it. I was tempted to highlight some passages of the book (especially the ones that explain that sex is not just about looking after only one person's needs) but I want him to experience his own epiphanies, so, I didn't. I'm hoping that he will take something from the book that can translate to our bedroom, something that helps make the sex act pleasurable for both of us.

I go to the kitchen to grab him a beer and when I come back I smile to the point of grinning. Martin is looking through the book like it's the most amazing thing that he's ever seen.

"Here's your beer, sweetie," I say and I smile even further when he can barely remove his eyes from the introduction. If we can make the physical thing work, there just might be hope for us.

My mother doesn't move from her spot in Doris' kitchen and as more people arrive, she greets them like the queen of the royal court whose subjects have come to pay their respects. I keep myself busy and helpful by making sure everybody has enough to eat and drink. Martin stays seated in the armchair the whole time and as he seems to be making good headway with the book, I don't want to unseat him and introduce him to people he doesn't know or will never see again.

When Steve, Janice and Stacy arrive, only Steve

gives me a warm welcome and looks happy to see me. Janice gives me a cursory acknowledgement but lights up when she greets my mom, who makes room for her to sit beside her, as if they are the best of friends.

Doris seems conspicuously absent and when I go out back I see her sitting in a lawn chair. Staring mindlessly into space, in one hand she has a lit cigarette and a beer in the other. I've never seen her so down in the mouth before and her state of depression, if that's what it is, concerns me. I want her to confide in me. I want to offer her some assistance or insight or sympathy or whatever it is that she so desires to make her feel better.

I have a lot of life experience and I think that I could help her with some guidance or advice, or even share a 'for instance,' if she would only open up to me and not treat me like I'm some kind of airhead that only merits her pity.

"Mom seems to be enjoying herself," I say as I grab two beers from a tub of ice-cold beer by the door and sit in a chair beside her.

"She loves the attention," Doris says.

"She deserves it," I say.

"Why does she deserve it?" she asks and her question throws me.

"It's her birthday," I say. "It's her seventieth," I add, just to further justify the attention I think she deserves. Doris doesn't seem too convinced, however and turns her head back around. I sense that she wants me to say something that she needs to hear me say but it's killing me that I don't know exactly what that is. No way am I going with an apology again.

"Life goes by so quick, doesn't it?" she asks, still looking ahead.

"It sure does," I agree and I'm wondering if it's aging that's getting her so down.

"You're right to be dating someone so young," she says and her statement surprises me into silence. "The older people get, the more... cynical they become," she continues. "People get hard the more they age... angrier. Have you noticed?"

"Yes," I agree. "More set in their ways."

"I'm not talking about set in their ways, I'm talking anger. Disillusionment maybe leading to anger but people get angry as they age, like they get really, really angry and some of them don't even know it. They take it out on everyone around them but they don't even know themselves that they're angry."

"I think that's very true," I say, wondering if she's talking about herself, someone close to her or people in general.

"Maybe we get disillusioned and disappointed because we realize that, as our years get fewer and fewer, we're not going to get all the things that we thought we wanted when we were younger. It's like the clock is ticking down and there's less and less time to get what we want and some things that we wanted, we'll never get. It's like that train has left the station, you know?"

"Yes," I say encouragingly, hoping that she'll keep talking and get out all of what is on her mind.

"It's too late for me to become an astronaut, right? That just can't happen for me now."

"You wanted to be an astronaut?" I ask, trying to remember if this is the first time she's mentioning it.

"No, dummy. I'm using that as an example," she says, annoyed.

"Yes, I'm sorry. Some things we are excluded from just by being too old now."

"Last time Janice was up, she brought some friends and I hung out with them for a bit," she says and I'm trying to remember when that might have been. Did someone forget to tell me about that?

"It was a blast. Just sitting with them, talking shit… it made me feel young again, you know? Like, just being with them reminded me of what I was like when I was their age. It's a totally different mindset. I didn't give a fart about aging back then; never gave it a second thought, as if I considered myself ageless. I didn't give a shit about anything much, as a matter of fact, except maybe where we were going that night and did I have money to buy food with enough left over to get a really good buzz going in the bar."

"That takes me back," I say.

"I understand why you'd want to be with someone young. When you hang out with someone young long enough, you start to forget about all the shit you don't want to think about. Maybe you begin to think that you can be an astronaut, after all, and just because you're feeling angry, it doesn't mean that you're getting old."

"I hear you," I say when there's a lull but it takes me a while to try and decode what Doris is saying. I'm not actually sure I understand what point she's making and I hesitate to agree or disagree for fear of getting it wrong and making her angry again.

"We should go back in," she then says, standing.

As we return to the kitchen I notice my mom looking at us both with interest. She looks concerned, as if she maybe she thinks that we're scheming up some surprise for her that she's not going to like. I give her a twirly-finger wave as if to allay her fears and communicate that nothing bad is happening. My gesture doesn't seem to translate very well as her concerned expression doesn't change.

When I bring another beer to Martin, he's still sitting in the same chair. The book remains closed on his lap and I'm not sure what he has being doing for amusement since he finished with it. I hate to think that he's having a bad time at the party so I suggest that maybe he will have more fun if he mingled for a bit.

Ronald arrives and standing at the front door, looks around to get his bearings. As I go to greet him, his mood brightens at the sight of me.

"You made it," I say, receiving the bottle of wine he extends towards me.

"It's so good to see you," he says, sounding like he means it. "I'm having a horrible time."

"Did you bring Frank?" I ask, wondering if we were waiting or if we should move inside.

"It's over," Ronald says. "For good, this time."

"That's awful," I say as I lead him toward the kitchen. "Come tell me about it."

"It's like when we're apart we get on so well together..." he says, pausing as some guests push past us.

"What can I get you to drink? Wine?" I ask.

"Yes, please. But as soon as we get to spend some time together, in person, it's like we we're all weird with each other, like we don't even know what to say to each other, do you know that way?" Ronald says excitedly.

"Yes, I know exactly," I agree as I hand him a glass of Merlot.

"Then we argued and for the life of me, I don't even know what we were arguing about. He was like, accusing me of not trusting him. He thought that I was thinking that he was cheating and that he couldn't be trusted and he said that that was one of the most crucial things for him in a relationship, like I think he said it was a deal breaker and, I don't know, it just got real weird..."

"So you left?"

"Well, not right away, I'm giving the Cliff notes here.

We both got so angry that one of us had to leave or we would have ended in fisticuffs… well, probably not but we would have said some stuff that we could never take back, it was just going to a really weird place, like he was so over-the-top paranoid."

"Does he do drugs?" I ask softly.

"No, I don't think so. He may be on some prescription meds for depression and stuff but it was too soon to have that conversation."

I don't want to get pin holed in the corner of the kitchen hearing all about Ronald's failed romance so as Chuck passes by, I grab him. "Hey, Chuck, have you met my good friend, Ronald?"

"No, I don't think I have," Chuck says, leaning back to get a good look at Ronald's face. "How do you do?" he says, extending his hand.

"I'll be right back," I say as I dash off and go look for Martin.

Martin's armchair is empty so my intuition tells me that he finally needed to pee, what with all the beer he's been drinking. As I climb the stairs and turn the corridor I see him in line for the bathroom.

"Who are the hep cat swingers?" he asks me, referring to Steve and Stacy who are walking back towards the outside stairs. His jaw almost drops when I tell him that Steve is my ex-husband. For a few seconds he stands exhibiting what appears to be shock. I don't feel like getting into a past history discussion right now and luckily for me the bathroom door opens. As we watch an elderly woman slowly exit the bathroom, I give him a kiss on the cheek and say, "See you later," as he scurries inside.

I collect whatever empty glasses and beer bottles that I can and return to the kitchen. Ronald isn't talking to Chuck anymore and when he sees me reenter, he follows me around as I do some more collecting and cleaning.

"I booked this Bed and Breakfast but it's too late now to cancel it," he says and I'm not sure what kind of a response he's expecting from me.

"That's messed up," I say as I dredge the remaining drops of beer from two beer bottles into the sink.

"I mean, what's the point of me staying around by myself?"

"I know."

"Even if he did call me and apologize, I'm not going to... I'm so over it at this point."

"It's a pity you guys couldn't work through it," I say as I empty a trash can into a garbage bag.

"You think we could have patched things up?" he asks with a sudden sense of urgency. "Was I too rash in walking out like that?"

"You probably did all that you could, Ronald. You guys have been at odds from the beginning, it sounds like. I wouldn't beat yourself up over it."

"Yeah," he says thinking, as I brush past him to rinse my sticky fingers in the sink.

"Did you meet my mom?"

"No, but... I'm fine, she's busy," he says as he looks over at the group of neighbors and friends that surround my mother.

"Maybe you can join us in singing Happy Birthday?" I say as I see that Doris is lighting the candles on the birthday cake.

"I can do that," Ronald says.

After we all sing Happy Birthday to my mother, I help cut the cake and place many slices on individual plates in order to share them out among the guests. I try to pass off Ronald to anyone that I can but he doesn't seem too keen on mixing with anyone but me. What does he want from me, exactly? Maybe I'm too soft and I should toughen up a bit like my mom and my sister. They wouldn't let him sing his 'poor me' song without calling him on his shit. Why can't I do that?

I haven't seen Martin in a while so I decide to go look for him. Steve and Stacy are ready to go and they ask me whether I know if Janice was going with them or going to crash here. Steve is such a sweetheart that he says he'll book a room for Janice at the motel that they're staying at, if she wants to stay with them.

I find Martin in the office. Janice is sitting on the sofa beside him and is, presumably, getting his feedback on her student film which is playing on the TV. I admire Martin for being willing to give his opinion but I especially appreciate Janice for looking after Martin, who I'm sure has been bored out of his skull the entire evening. Then it occurs to me to wonder why she wanted Martin's opinion in the first place. "There you are," I say to Martin as I stand at the doorway.

"I'm showing Martin my short," Janice says, as if I'm interrupting. "You don't have a problem with me entertaining your boyfriend, do you?" she asks in a tone which I'm not sure was meant to sound bratty or not.

Martin looks totally baffled by my exchange with Janice and I'm wondering if she even mentioned to him that she's my daughter. I'm not surprised when she decides to leave and go with Steve rather than sleep over here but I am still confused about why she seems particularly interested in what Martin thinks of her film.

"Take care of the DVD for me and I'll pick it up tomorrow, okay?" she says kindly to Martin. "We can talk about it then."

"You bet," Martin says and I can tell by his expression that he's feeling very uncomfortable. My guess is that he hates what he's seen of her film already and I've no doubt that her coldness to me doesn't go unnoticed by him. A weird bedroom scene remains frozen on the TV screen. "You don't have to watch the rest," I half-whisper when Janice leaves the room.

"Are you guys related?" he asks straight away.

"Janice is my daughter," I say and I can see the wheels turning in his head.

"Steve is her father?" he asks.

"No, I never kept in touch with her father," I tell him.

"You never said that you had a twenty-year-old daughter," he says, looking very confused.

"You said that you wanted things to be revealed as we went along, right?"

"You were married twice?" he asks.

Taking Martin's hands in mine, I sit beside him on the sofa and I tell him about having Janice when I was eighteen and about Steve and about my second marriage and how that didn't work out. I don't go into details about anything as I'm sure if on the slim chance that we do have a future together, there will be plenty of times for more in-depth discussion.

"I did marry someone since Steve but that didn't end well. Let's save that story for another day, what do you think?" I suggest.

"That's a lot to digest and I honestly don't know what to think," Martin says.

"Welcome to my life," I say as I give a wry smile. When I kiss the back of Martin's right hand, his face brightens considerably. "We're sleeping in here tonight, okay? Enjoy the movie," I say as I get up to leave.

When I return to the party, most guests have gone home. I admit to wanting the evening to be over already as I collect some empty beer bottles.

"I'm heading to bed, sis. I'm pooped," Doris says as I meet her by the stairs. "Chuck is going to stay up and make sure anyone that's left is doing okay. It's just mom and a couple of her cronies. And your boss. What a dweeb."

"He's not really... I guess, he is kinda my boss," I correct myself. "Good night," I say, as sis climbs the stairs.

When I get back to the kitchen, mom is chatting to the last two party guests. I get the impression that she really doesn't want her special evening to end.

"There you are," Ronald says as he enters the kitchen from out back. What was he doing in the back yard? "Do you think I should call him?" he asks.

"Call who? Oh, Frank? It's a bit late, isn't it?" I say, feeling like I'm done with his whole drama.

"He won't be asleep. You think I should wait for him to call me? Calling him is like as admission, isn't it? That I was the one in the wrong?"

"You know what, Ronald?" I say, feeling some of my sister's straight shooting style rub off on me. "It's been a long day and this is my mom's birthday party. When I invited you it was for you guys to come and have some fun..."

"I'm having a crisis, Frances," Ronald protests.

"Ronald, with all due respect, you've been in crisis with this guy since the day you met him. I'm your work colleague, not an agony aunt or something."

"Fine," Ronald says, thinking. "What's an agony aunt?"

"A relationship know-it-all, an advice columnist," I say. Ronald looks at me as if to say, 'What's gotten into the Frances I know and love?'

"Are you okay?" he asks.

"Yes, I'm okay, Ronald. I just have enough on my

plate without having to listen to your dating drama, that's all. It would be nice if you asked me how I'm doing every once in a while or, better still, what if we didn't share our personal stuff at all and just confined our contact to a working relationship, if it's all the same to you."

Ronald looks at me like I just slapped him in the face or something. As he puts down his drink, I can almost see him composing some choice parting words in his head.

"I'm sorry I've become such a nuisance to you," he says, grabbing his jacket. "I won't bother you again," he says and storms off into the night.

I don't feel like running after him to apologize because I don't feel at all sorry. I actually feel a relief wash over me, as if I finally had the guts to tell him how I've been feeling, all along. So what if I get fired?

I realize that I'm reluctant to go join Martin in the makeshift bed in the office and I realize that part of the reason is that I don't particularly feel like another night of awkwardness and bad sex. I actually desire to be alone and I'm thinking that maybe I'll find someplace else in the house to crash. Pouring myself a final glass of wine — and promising myself that it's the last one — I walk out into the back yard to merge my lonesome spirit with the dark beauty and stillness of the night.

As I look up at the night sky, I fully take in the gorgeous exquisiteness and sheer majesty of the star-filled universe above and beyond us. Seeing the immense beauty and clarity of the twinkling silver stars, I'm reminded, once again, of how living in the city for all these years has deprived me of such a wondrous view.

As I sit in a deck chair and peer straight upwards, I wonder what my life would have been like had I never left here for LA. Did I lose something by leaving here so young? Did I leave a part of myself behind? Did I lose or gain anything by leaving my family behind?

I feel so estranged from my kin and yet when we get together, we don't even feel like family. I don't feel loved and accepted by my mother and sister; at best, I feel like they just about tolerate me and don't at all think about me or miss me when we're not together. Should I move back up and try to fit myself back in? I am lost in thought when my mother comes outside.

"It's lovely out here at night, isn't it?" my mother says as she sits in a lawn chair beside me. "They've all gone home; it's just you and me now."

"Did you have a nice party?" I ask.

"It was wonderful," my mom says and I can see that she totally loved it and probably wished that it had gone on longer. Are we all basically lost and lonely creatures, starved of attention, no matter what age we are?

"You don't want to go to bed?" she asks.

"I miss seeing the stars, momma. In LA when I look up at night, all I see is the murky haze of yellow and orange smog. Not a star to be seen anywhere."

"That's probably just what hell looks like," my mom says and laughs. "I'd appreciate it if, when you get back there, if you don't tell anyone. Any more people relocate here from LA and they'll just turn this place into the same place they're trying to escape from... just a matter of time."

"Why didn't you marry again, mom, after dad left us? You've been alone all these years."

"As long as you surround yourself with friends and community, sweetie, you'll never be alone. Besides, I have two beautiful daughters. Why would I get married again?"

"Don't you miss...?

"No, Frances, I don't. I felt more alone being with your father than when I was without him. Just because you have a man, doesn't mean that you won't feel all alone.

Being with someone and feeling like that can be much worse than being all by yourself. Besides, who said I've been without a man all these years, anyways?" my mom asks and even though it's dark, I can still see a twinkle in her eyes.

"I don't want to know, momma, but I'm glad. I'm glad that you didn't give up."

"Is that what you feel like, sweetie? Giving up?"

"Sometimes I feel like I can't do it anymore... be with someone, all the time."

"Then don't. Who says you have to be with the same man all the time? And whoever tells you that you should, don't listen to them. Be alone, be with someone, be with someone else, who gives a rat's ass? It's your happiness. It's your life. You gotta make the best of it. Who cares what it looks like to others?"

"I wish it were that easy, momma," I say wistfully.

"It is, sweetheart. It really is. It's only a problem when we think about things too much and over-complicate everything. It's our expectations of how we think things should be that makes us unhappy."

My mom looks at me and I'm sure that she can tell from my facial expression that I'm thinking about what she just said. "Life is what it is, sweetheart," she continues. "We complicate things and make ourselves unhappy when we fight what is and expect it to be different. I'm going to bed," she says and gives me a really warm and caring hug. "Don't pay any attention to what Doris says," she whispers, "she hasn't been herself since the miscarriage."

When I turn to face my mom more fully, the shocked look on my face tells her that I didn't know. "She didn't tell you? Well, you didn't hear it from me, then," she says, as if she could kick herself for letting the cat out of the bag. "Seriously," she says, as if fearing the worst if the truth got out, "you didn't hear that from me."

Unable to respond in any adequate fashion, I watch my mom make a hasty retreat and quickly vanish inside the house. Her sudden absence leaves me with a sense of shock and I feel tiny and insignificant in the dark, still night searching for meaning beneath a canopy of distant stars and other remote planetary worlds.

CHAPTER 14

I'm so revved up to see Martin again that I walk quickly and silently through the now-quiet house. I want to see his face and hear his laugh so badly that I'm going to wake him up, even if he is tired and deeply asleep. I want to be held by him and feel his hot breath on my neck and feel his soft skin against my naked body. We don't have to have sex; in fact, what I'm truly craving is closeness and connection. I want to look into his eyes and fully appreciate the way that he looks at me; the unique and individual way that he sees me.

As I enter the darkened room, Martin comes rushing to greet me. As if he hasn't seen me for months, he hugs me so tight I can barely breathe. "Wow, somebody missed me," I say.

"Oh, I missed you," he says, sounding upset. "Don't ever leave me again."

"What's going on?" I ask as I hold his shoulders to get a look at his face.

"What's going on?" he says, as if he has a list and he doesn't know where to start. "All your friends are weirdness personified: your ex-husband is a pervert, your daughter is a pornographer and your sister's husband is having an affair."

"Chuck is having an affair?" I ask in half-whispered outrage. When Martin tells me that Chuck came into the office and thinking that it was empty, he made a phone sex call to a mistress, I don't believe him. I don't know why Martin would make up such a story; he did drink a lot of beers; does he make stuff up when he drinks?

"If you don't believe me, hit redial," Martin says as he picks up the office phone. "See who answers. If you get her machine, you've got a name and a number. Case closed."

Figuring that the worst case scenario was that I'd wake somebody up (in which case I'd say, 'wrong number'), I held the phone to my ear and pressed redial. Hands on his hips, Martin looks at me expectantly, as if his vindication is at hand. "Hello?" a female voice answers.

"Hello," I say, "who is this, please?"

"Is that you, Frances?" she asks and in an instant, my voice switches instantly from suspicious to familiar.

"Oh, hi, Doris. It's Frances. I know it's late but we can't find the pillows," I quickly improvise.

"Everything should be behind the sofa. If you're missing anything, there's extra bedding in the hall closet."

"Oh, Martin found them. Sorry for disturbing you."

When I hang up, Martin's puzzled expression looks even more bewildered. "Chuck called his wife from the downstairs phone to have phone sex?" he asks like it's the craziest thing ever.

"I guess," I say, not wanting to get into my sister's private life. "If that's what you heard."

I can feel an excitement building up in me as we put the makeshift bed together: I'm actually looking forward to holding and being held by Martin. I realize then that he reminds me of Bailey, a little puppy that we used to have when I was a child. Martin seems so appreciative to be with me and he has such an excitable and fun energy, I feel like I want to play with him all the time, even when my mood is dark or sad.

"What did you think of the book?" I whisper into his ear as I spoon him beneath the covers.

"I liked it," he says and although I can't see his face, I know that just the thought of our togetherness has put a grin on his face.

"What did you like about it?" I ask, enjoying the tease.

"I like trying new things," he says and I can feel as his body becomes aroused.

"You want to try new things with me?" I ask seductively.

"Totally," he says and turns his body over towards mine.

From my limited understanding, tantric sex between two people is more about making an intimate connection with your partner than it is about having mind-blowing orgasms. In fact, couples can go for hours without either partner reaching orgasm at all. If the male partner does reach orgasm, the trick is for him to channel the sexual energy internally and not explode outwardly at all.

The original purpose was to make the sexual act between people be a more spiritual one and with enough practice, couples could actually reach high levels of spiritual awareness. I'm not expecting any of that with Martin, at least not right away, but if it does help him to slow down and not be so orgasm-fixated, that would be a helpful start.

"Does that feel good?" I ask as we're about five minutes into what I hope to be a long and slow night of physical and spiritual togetherness. We are caressing and stroking each other and I feel closer to him than ever. Maybe tantric will do the trick for us.

"It's more than good," he says, sounding like an out-of-breath weight-lifter. "It's amazing." His words and breath come faster and faster now. I realize that he is on the edge.

"Don't come!" I say as I sense his imminent release.

"What?" he manages to ask.

"Don't come. It's tantric. You read the book, right?"

"The text was so boring and confusing. I mostly just looked at the pictures."

171

"In tantric sex you reach orgasm without coming."

"What, now? Isn't that an oxymoron?" he says, breathing heavily, clearly excited.

"You circulate the energy internally, instead of letting it explode in orgasm."

"Too late," he says breathing hard and his body shudders as he explodes, his body tensing and then relaxing as he falls in a heap beside me.

"Are you okay?" I ask when he doesn't speak or move.

"I'm fine," he says, sounding like a drunken man who has just found out that he won the lottery. "How are you?" he asks after a long moment. I sigh.

As I fold up the sheets and bedding from our night in the office, I smile. Even though my first night ever of tantric sex was a disaster, I had fun and this is definitely one of those occasions to look back on and laugh.

"Leave everything as it is," Doris says as she walks in, still dressed in her robe. "I'll throw everything into the wash."

"Good morning," I say.

"Good morning," she replies as she hands me a colorful brochure. "This is the relationship seminar I was telling you about. The tickets are stapled to the back."

"Thanks," I say, taking a cursory look at it. "I doubt if I'll be going."

"Give it to one of your friends down there, I don't care. Where's Martin?"

"He's making us breakfast," I say and I can't help but smile.

"Chuck is making mine. What's so amusing?" Doris asks.

"It's been a long time since a man made me

breakfast," I admit.

"Bill never made you breakfast?" she asks incredulously.

"In all our years being married, Bill could never find the kitchen."

"That must have sucked," Doris says as she sits on the sofa.

"Yeah," I say, as I sit beside her and pull my legs up under me, "it did. Bill liked to think that he was so progressive and liberal, as far as equal treatment of women was concerned."

"He wasn't?"

"It's one thing to say it; it's another thing to practice it. It's funny the roles that we expect each other to play, when we get married."

"How do you mean?"

"I'm sure I'm just as guilty but he definitely believed that it was a woman's role to be in the kitchen."

"Eek, I hate that," Doris says.

"The first time I found out, it was a shock. Saturdays he liked to watch sports... I didn't know this till one day he plonked himself down in front of the TV, opened up his laptop, put his feet up, and asked me, 'What are we having for lunch, babe?'" I smile at the memory now but back then, it came as something of a rude awakening. "I didn't mind making him lunch; it was the expectation that somehow he assumed that that was my role. Kinda glad we didn't have kids."

"Don't you just love the balls on some guys? If Chuck tried to pull that shit, I'd tell him that the first thing to go is the TV. He'd be next. You're doing the right thing with Martin. Get them young and treat them rough, that's my motto."

"No, it isn't," I say and playfully shove my sister.

"You'd like to think that you're tough but you and I know you're just a big softie inside."

"The bane of my existence," Doris says and playfully pushes me back. "I must have inherited it from you. Definitely not from mom."

"Definitely not," I agree and we both laugh at a joke that only we would get, a hilarious moment arising out of our shared family history. I want desperately for my sister to tell me about her miscarriage so I can tell her how sorry I am and let her know that I love and support her and that she can count on me and she can call on me anytime… but she doesn't.

Perhaps now is not the time but, if I'm leaving soon, when will be the best time? Maybe it's not something that she wants to share with me, anyway. Possibly she's afraid that if she tells me, I'll only annoy her with my touchy-feely LA speak, as she puts it.

"Ah, breakfast," Doris exclaims as Martin and Chuck enter with dinner trays jam-packed with breakfast food. "Let's just all sit on the floor and have it here."

"Where is mom?" I ask, as if remembering that she stayed the night.

"She left early," Doris answers. "She didn't want to wake you guys so she told me to tell you thanks for everything."

"Cool," I say and I wonder if I'll get another chance to see her before I leave. It feels good to be spending time with my family and I'm beginning to miss them already. If I spent some more quality time up here, perhaps we could all get to know each other, all over again. I think I would like that.

After breakfast, I decide I want to spend some quality time with Martin and figure that I'll take him around to see all of my old haunts. As we walk into Fairfax and I take his hand, I feel like all is right in the world. It's a beautiful day and everything is so lush, fragrant and green, I feel like we're in paradise, Northern California style. I could live here.

"It's so green up here," Martin says, as if he was reading my mind as he looks around with appreciation. "It's so amazing to be seeing trees again. Didn't think I missed them until now."

"I know. I was just thinking that myself."

"I forget sometimes that in LA, we're actually living in a desert, basically," he says as he deeply fills his lungs with clean air. As I do the same, I think back on what my mom was saying: that life is what it is. It can sound so trite but I think I understand what she means; I think that that's the way I'm feeling right now: in this moment, walking hand in hand with Martin, everything seems perfect. And if it's not perfect, then it's okay.

"What are you thinking?" Martin asks, as I'm sure he's sensing some distance between us.

"Life is what it is," I answer. "It's something my mom told me last night."

"That's a saying I've heard younger kids use a lot," Martin says. "It is what it is. It's all good."

"Younger kids?" I ask, in jest.

"There are some younger people than me, Frances," Martin jokes back. "I think the generation behind me are reincarnated hippies, as a matter of fact; that's my theory, anyway. What else did your mom say?"

"She said that we make ourselves unhappy by not accepting life as it is; that it's our wanting to change life to how we *think* it should be that causes us problems."

"Your mom sounds very wise, grasshopper," Martin jokes.

"Do you think that it's the same with people, Martin?"

"Is what the same?"

"Maybe people only annoy us when we expect them to be different than they actually are. Like we expect our parents to be a certain way and when they're not, it makes us unhappy. Same in relationship... same for everybody in our lives, really."

"That would make sense, except that they are not really annoying us, per se. We are annoyed by them because they're not acting in a way that we think they should be acting, right?"

"I accept you as you are, Martin."

"You do?"

"I do. There's nothing about you that annoys me or that I feel like I need to change."

"Maybe that's why we're so perfect for each other. I totally accept you."

"You do?"

"I do."

"I'm not too... touchy-feely for you?"

"I don't know what that means but I love your touchy-feely. It's my favorite part of you. I can't get enough," he jokes and as we walk down the main street of Fairfax, I push him around, in jest.

"Keep that up and no touchy-feely for you," I joke in his 'grasshopper' accent.

Martin and I have the best time strolling around Fairfax; window shopping, stopping for coffee and ice cream and just generally goofing around. My head seems to get a vacation when I spend time with Martin; it's like I'm not thinking but just being. I don't think about Bill or my work or what I think is lacking in my life; as if another me comes out to play, with Martin, I just seem to have fun.

"Steve invited us to have dinner later today, I hope you don't mind?" I ask as we lick our individual ice cream cones. "Then we'll hit the road."

"I don't want this to end, Frances," Martin says and his expression doesn't make it clear to me if he's being serious or not.

"Me, neither," I say, seriously.

Steve chose a lovely French restaurant for us all to meet up in. As we sit around a table by the front window, I notice a coolness between Stacy and Janice. Perhaps it's not personal and Stacy is just annoyed that her time with Steve is being shared with someone else. Then again, maybe Janice just doesn't like anybody.

"Order whatever you girls want," Steve says, "...and Martin," he adds with a smirk on his face. I can tell that Martin isn't at all sure about Steve. He looks at him as if he's wondering if the guy is for real. I admit that Steve doesn't help his case much, what with bad jokes that all seem to have a double meaning.

"I'll get mine and Frances," Martin says and I know right away that arguing over paying for stuff is a guy thing. One look at the exorbitant prices on the menu and I know that Martin can't really afford this.

"Martin, let Steve get this one," I say. "He did invite us and I know him well enough to know that he'd feel very insulted if we didn't accept his gracious hospitality."

"Yes, I would," Steve agrees. "You can get the next one, kid."

I see Martin wince at the word, 'kid,' and I can almost hear him say to himself that there will be no next time. "What is everybody having?" I ask, hoping to draw their attention away from each other and back to the menu.

"Do you have to speak French to eat here?" Janice asks, referring to how the menu is all in French.

"I'm in the mood for a bit of Blanc de Poulet," Steve says.

"What's that?" asks Janice.

"Chicken breast," answers Stacy.

"I'm a breast man in any language," Steve says, grinning.

"That would make you a Blanc man in France," Stacy says, joining in. Not at all amused, Janice looks at me and gives me her, 'I could throw up right now' look.

Martin's mood doesn't recover from his interaction with Steve and all through the meal, he says very little and looks like he can't wait to get this rendezvous over with. Even when the meal finally ends and we get back into the car to drive back to LA, Martin seems so distant that I get the sense that he is still angry about something.

"What are you thinking?" I ask him as we drive the secondary roads on the way to the freeway.

"I can't believe that you have a twenty-year-old daughter and that you were married to that guy Steve and then you were married again to some mysterious dude, whose name you don't even dare mention," he says with a scowl.

Wow, I almost say out loud.

"What are you doing with me?" he asks. "What is this, you and me? Why are you dating someone so young, I mean, comparatively young?"

"I'm not dating you because you're young, Martin. I'm dating you because I like you."

"I think you're dating me because... I don't know why you're dating me. I don't think you're taking this seriously... taking me seriously, at all. It's like you're just, I don't know, biding your time 'till something better comes along."

As I pull over to the side of the road to stop the car,

178

I'm wondering where all this insecurity is coming from. Looking at it from his point of view, I'm sure that it must look like I'm not taking him very seriously, as a mate. Yet, at the same time, there's nothing I've said or done to make him feel like I'm not taking him seriously, as a person. Does he subconsciously know that, as we drive back to LA, I'm not expecting to be seeing him again?

"Of course I take you seriously," I say. "I wouldn't have invited you to meet my family if I wasn't serious about you. I don't take boyfriends to visit my family, Martin. I didn't say anything but taking you home was a big deal for me."

"I didn't know that," Martin says, his anger shifting considerably. "I didn't know it was a big deal."

"I'm not playing with you, sweetie," I say softly, "if that's what you're worried about. I like you a whole lot."

"You do?"

"Yes, I do," I say and as I look into Martin's big brown soulful eyes, my heart almost skips a beat. I do feel for him like a lover and not as a mother; well, maybe a little bit as a mother. If I feel protective towards him it's because I feel protective towards his innocence and his naiveté, which, because I have it so much in abundance within myself, I recognize.

Dr. Roberts says that we have reactions to other people because they remind us of aspects of ourselves; we like or don't like some other person because that person reflects back to us some aspect of ourselves that we may or may not like. Maybe when I feel protective towards Martin, in some way, I'm feeling protective towards myself.

As I place my hand against his soft face, I feel like I owe it to him — owe it to both of us — to maybe give this my best shot and not discount him because of his age and lack of experience in the bedroom.

179

Do I really care what other people think? Do I care that Doris and my mom and Steve all secretly think that we don't have a hope and a prayer? No one makes me feel the way Martin makes me feel. Who am I to toss that away so casually, without first seeing it all the way through? Martin is who he is and he came into my life for a reason. Right now, I'm not sure exactly what that reason is but as Dr. Roberts told me, spend enough time with a person and relationships have a way of coming to their natural state of affairs, all by themselves.

"I want to invite you to a relationship seminar that's starting next week," I tell him as I pull out the brochure that Doris gave to me. I'm beginning to believe Dr. Roberts when she says that there are no coincidences in life. When Doris gave me the tickets, I considered then that I had no use for them. Now, I'm seeing how perfect it all is.

Going to a relationship seminar with Martin would help to position us in a way that perhaps nothing else could, at this stage. Almost like a bench test for our relationship, our participation may determine if we do have a future or not.

"A relationship seminar? Seriously? Isn't that just for morons?" Martin asks.

"You've got nothing to learn?"

"I learn as I go. Like most people."

"Sometimes it helps to know beforehand what to expect, don't you think? It's like, if you knew there was a mountain up ahead, you could bring some supplies, some rope or something."

"If you knew there was mountain in the way, you'd stay home and watch TV and maybe watch someone else climb it on the Discovery Channel or something..." He shrugs, looking confused and then adds, "I don't know what we're talking about."

"I got pregnant at eighteen, married at twenty. I don't regret having Janice but I sure as heck would have preferred to have had that parental talk before I left the house."

"So, what you're saying is that you don't want to leap until you know what it is that you're leaping into? I mean with all the books you read and these seminars and stuff…you're trying to… minimize your risk?"

"I'm trying to learn. I'm trying to have better, more successful relationships… to understand better and not keep fucking up one relationship after another. Do you have the relationship thing all worked out? There's nothing you need to learn or understand better?"

"Can I ask you a question?" Martin asks, as he looks over the brochure.

"Sure."

"Do you want to have a successful relationship with me?"

"Yes," I answer.

"You want to be in love with me and be loved by me?"

"Again, yes."

"Well, then we're arguing about the same thing except you think we have to read books and go to seminars and stuff, when all we have to do is… just do it!"

"Do what?"

"Fall in love."

"Is that what you want, Martin? You want to fall in love with me? You want us to fall in love?"

"I'll tell you exactly what I want," Martin says as he turns his body more fully towards mine, takes my hands into his and looks me straight and hard in the eyes. "I want to feel the joy and the mystery and the passion of being in love. I want to stare into my lover's eyes for hours and hours. I want to feel her skin against mine and caress it like it was the most precious thing in the world. I want to go somewhere I've never been before, somewhere so new... it's going to blow my mind and I would love to go there with you, Frances."

I stare at him, trying to process what he said.

"That's so beautiful, Martin," I say and I know that although Martin may think that he's being authentic, what he sounds like to me is someone that's quoting lines from a movie. I'm just as guilty in once having believed that movie love is real love but real life is not the movies.

"Thank you," Martin says, his head nodding sagely, as if, in his head, he's taking a well-deserved bow.

"But I'm not your happiness. And you're not mine. What you're describing, you have to find within yourself or in your work or something."

Martin's jaw actually drops and he looks at me like I just threw a bucket of ice cold water all over him, which, metaphorically, I guess I did.

CHAPTER 15

Once on the freeway, we cruise back towards Los Angeles traveling 70 miles an hour in complete silence. Unusually for me, I don't want to listen to any music and I don't want to engage in conversation; not that Martin looks particularly keen to chat as he stares listlessly out the passenger door window.

Am I being unreasonable?

My next session with Dr. Roberts is days away but I wish I could get her on speakerphone now so I could talk everything through. What words of wisdom would she impart to me? What questions would she challenge me with?

Am I acting from a place of love and assurance or from a place of fear?

What really bites is that if I were a guy, I wouldn't be thinking twice about any of this; I'd be jumping right in, penis first. Does anybody believe that Steve tortures himself with questions of self-doubt every time he goes on a date with Stacy? Honestly, if he proposed and she said yes, he'd drive her straight to Vegas before she had a chance to change her mind. Once there, he'd do his best to get her pregnant in order to really seal the deal.

Is it just the age thing that I'm worried about? In fairness to Martin, it's something that he's aware of too, it's not like he doesn't know my history and how old I am. I probably should apologize for going off on him, like that. By saying no, I'm making a decision for both of us; is that being fair to Martin? If I say no to Martin, am I cheating us both out of a shot at love and happiness? If so, what kind of a life am I going back to, anyway?

It's not Martin's fault that things are as they are... and that's just it: things are as they are. I'm not sure that that realization helps any, actually... thanks anyway, mom.

What's happening here is that I'm saying no to love.

So what if the guy is younger or older? I didn't hesitate with Bill and despite the fact that he was older, I didn't think twice about it. I didn't think twice about it — not because of his age — but because back then I wasn't thinking about what it would feel like to fall out of love. I didn't even consider that I could get my heart broken. Even though, yes, Jim Costas had broken my heart years earlier, when I got involved with Bill, I never once considered that I could end up alone, broken-hearted and in misery.

It may not be Bill's fault but, rightly or wrongly, I've been in misery for longer than I care to remember; longer than anyone else seems to consider a 'reasonable' amount of time for someone to suffer from a broken heart. I don't know why it is but maybe some people are hurt more deeply from disappointments in love and take longer to recover. I know that I fudge the years of my separation and divorce from Bill because I don't want people to judge me as being emotionally weak and feeble. It's bad enough to be twice divorced.

What have I got to lose from taking another chance on love? No, I hear the voice of Dr. Roberts saying to me, that's not the question; the question is: what have you got to *gain* from taking another chance on love?

"I guess I'm just scared," I say out loud and Martin jumps slightly, as if by breaking the silence, I spooked him. "I can blame all the ex-husbands and ex-boyfriends that I want but I really haven't been very good at relationship. It's been one train wreck after another. I must really suck at relationship."

Martin looks at me with what I can only describe as a mix of puzzlement and excitement.

"If I could give up on relationship altogether and be happy, I would, but I know that I wouldn't be happy alone, just by myself. I do want what you want, I do, I'm just…terrified," I say.

"Maybe you shouldn't be so hard on yourself," he says. "I think most people are scared inside."

"Are you, Martin? Do you feel scared inside?"

"No. I don't think so."

"And you really want to be in love with me?" I ask, wanting him to convince me all over again.

"Yes. Yes, I do."

"You want to stare at me while I sleep and… run through the poppy fields playing catch and kiss and have mad passionate sex in every room and every nook and cranny of the house?" I ask, prompting him with classic movie clichés.

"All of the above, yes!"

"Then let's do it," I finally say. "Let's fall in love!"

"Just like that?" he asks.

"Just like that!"

"I'm excited but to be honest, I didn't know that falling in love was a decision we need to make?" he says but it sounds more like a question.

"To adopt the Zen mind is to be conscious of everything you do. That includes falling in love," I say, hoping to recover for myself the calm wisdom of the Zen book.

"In every room and every nook and cranny, I like it!" he says, almost licking his lips with expectation.

"I've got a few days before I start my next project. Let's spend some serious time together, just you and me. Let's be carefree and silly, what do you say?" I ask, my

185

mood becoming cheerful again.

"Okay!"

"And next weekend we'll do the relationship seminar. Deal?"

"Deal."

The next few days I spend with Martin feels like bliss personified. I enjoy more romantic moments with Martin in a few short days than I have in the past ten years; it's as heady as all get out. One of the most amazing and perhaps shocking aspects to spending time like this with Martin is that I rediscovered my own neighborhood all over again. Even though I've lived in Santa Monica for almost two decades, we explore so much of it together that it's as if I'm seeing it for the very first time.

Even though the Ferris wheel (and the Santa Monica Pier, in general) is as iconic to the city as say the Eiffel Tower is to Paris, I never rode on it, until now. Living so close to the ocean, one would assume that I spend a lot of time on its sandy beaches but over the years, the sunset walks along the shore have become fewer and fewer. Not only did Martin and I take a stroll along the surf's edge every evening — and sometimes morning, too — but I actually got into the water for a swim; something I haven't done in such a long time.

We rent bikes and ride on the bike path which runs along the beach. We don't make the full 26 miles but we do bike long and hard enough to commiserate with each other the next day when our bums and leg muscles are so sore we can hardly get out of bed; not that staying in bed all day is a problem for either of us.

As we hike in the Santa Monica Mountains, Martin gets his chance to chase me through the poppy fields... well, they aren't exactly fields of golden poppies, just some hardy desert grasses and sage bushes... but we still have a blast, regardless. Hand in hand we meander through the Third Street Promenade, licking ice cream cones as we stop every now and then to watch the street performers. It is really magical. I lean back against him, his arms wrapped around me, and we listen to the musicians play.

Being alone for so long, I'd almost forgotten what it was like to have a companion to do fun things with. It's almost as if, being single, I excluded myself from doing things and going places because I didn't consider going by myself. I thought that I was being brave dining in restaurants alone but that's really just the tip of the solo experience iceberg. There's such a vast world to experience out there. Being with Martin opens my eyes up to greater possibilities.

Our togetherness has also put a spotlight on the small world that I had been living and choosing for myself up to this point. Seeing greater promise for myself in a more expansive world seems like it could be a reflection of my heart opening up again. Maybe my heart being so constricted, almost turned in on itself, for such a long time, affected how I looked at the world, in general. Could a small heart, mean a small vision?

The more time I spend with Martin, the more I'm beginning to believe again. I'm beginning to believe again that all things are possible. I'm beginning to believe again that true happiness is attainable and can last to the end of our days. I'm beginning to regain my appetite for trying new things; experiencing new things; experiencing as much as I possibly can.

I want to see more; I want to travel. I want us to go to Europe together. What a thrill we could have, taking small fishing boats to trek around the tiny islands of Greece. Maybe Martin could finance our trip to Borneo or some far-flung place by securing a commission with National Geographic or some other magazine that rewards glossy pictures taken in foreign lands. I'm not too old to go back-packing through South America or even just camping and hiking through the national parks in North America could be tremendous fun.

"I love you, Frances," Martin says as we lie on the floor of my living room, surrounded by pillows and wine glasses. We just ate the most gorgeous Chinese takeout and even though it is a hot and sunny day outside, we pulled the blinds, lit candles and set the air conditioner to freezing cold so that we could light a fire in the fireplace that hasn't been used since I moved here over ten years ago.

Martin stops massaging my foot when he realizes that his object of affection appears to be in total and utter shock. How can he say that he loves me when we barely even know each other? Why on earth would he go and spoil what has been an outrageously pleasurable past few days by throwing a spanner in the works with this grossly ill-timed declaration of love?

What on earth does this young pup know of love? Does he secretly want to sabotage everything that we have and everything that we could be together? Just when he was actually winning me over; opening my heart to him and the world... he pulls this shit? What a friggin' idiot!

I feel myself shut down and quickly withdraw into myself as if I have to circle the wagons to protect my heart. Like a new-born foal, my heart feels like it's very shaky on its trembling legs and now, just as it is barely born, it feels threatened. Martin looks at me with what looks like fear and shock in his eyes. He knows that he just blew it but he doesn't say anything to take it back, apologize or do something to fix it and make it right. He just stares at me, as if he expects me to fix things; just like Bill, he expects me to clean up after his mess.

I feel foolish, like I've made a fool of myself, yet again. I put myself out there and what do I get: a young kid whose only experience and knowledge of love comes from the aggregate of movies that he's seen.

Did I bring this down upon myself? Maybe the age thing is a major handicap, after all. Maybe I can only be with someone who knows love; someone who knows what it's like to have their heart broken; someone who knows pain.

This is all my fault. Two seconds ago I was on top of the world; now I'm feeling like I want to crawl into my bed and get beneath the covers and stay there. I'm reminded of that guy I used to work with, Vernon, who basically told me that I act like I'm not responsible for my own happiness. What he was trying to tell me was that I always seem to need someone else to make me happy. I guess that would make me co-dependent. I didn't want to hear him but then again maybe he is right, after all.

"All I've ever imagined that I could have from a girlfriend is understanding... to be understood," Martin says, perhaps realizing that I'm not okay with his premature declaration. "That she'd know me. Not the little things like my favorite color or something but that she could really see me for who I am. I feel like I have all that with you."

I don't know what to say to Martin; what do you say to someone who thinks that they're in love with you after just a handful of dates? I can't say no because that would break his heart and I can't say yes because that would be a lie. When Dr. Roberts doesn't want to answer a question with yes or no, she gives me a, 'For instance.'

"I bumped into an old friend of mine on the street the other day, some guy I used to work with," I begin as I start to tell him about what Vernon had said to me. I convey the theme of the conversation as best I can and then I sum up. "I don't want to be that person anymore," I eventually conclude.

Martin looks at me like I'm a crazy person or maybe he's so mad inside that I didn't say 'I love you' back that he secretly wants to hurt me; it's hard to tell from the mix of puzzlement and pain that's showing on his face. "What person?" he asks angrily. "I don't know what you're talking about."

I've never been so relieved to hear the front doorbell ring than at this very moment.

"Are you expecting someone?" Martin asks and in lieu of answering I jump right up and go to the door.

"It's Ronald," I almost say with glee as I look through the peephole.

"You're letting him in?" I hear Martin ask as I pull the door open. As the glaring sun hits my eyes, I feel like what a person under hypnosis might feel like when the hypnotist clicks their fingers and says, "Wake up!"

"Wow, it's dark in here," Ronald says as he kisses my cheek in greeting. "You've got a fire going?" he asks incredulously. "It's nearly triple digits out there!"

As I close the door and turn, as if a trance has been broken, I now can see what Ronald is seeing: madness. Despite the fact that it is the middle of the day in sunny Southern California, the living room looks like the movie version of a wood cabin in the Swiss Alps.

"Sorry for showing up like this," Ronald says, "but I've left you like six messages on your voicemail and the client's seriously freaking out about the changes."

"What changes?" I ask as I feel myself coming back to normal. Like the enchantment I have been under these past few days has finally broken, I can feel myself returning to the person that Ronald is more familiar with.

"Yeah, that was voicemail message number one,"

he says as he takes out the new sketches and blueprints.

"I'll put on some coffee," I say as I urgently desire a sober brain that caffeine can help provide. As I go to the kitchen to prepare some hot water for the coffee, I remember that Martin must be around somewhere. I find him in the bedroom. He's dressing himself so quickly that the buttons on his shirt are mismatched.

"Martin, I'm so sorry, I have to deal with this. It's work, okay?"

"You didn't even introduce us," he says angrily, packing his duffle bag and not even looking at me.

"Martin, the past few days have been real fun but we can't cocoon ourselves away from the world and live in some little love bubble forever. I have to deal with this, okay?"

"Yeah, well guess what?" he says petulantly. "I think our little love bubble just burst."

Martin walks straight past me and is out the front door so quickly, I don't have time to consider an appropriate response. I'm not surprised that he might feel a bit peeved by the interruption but I am surprised by the immature way that he's handling himself.

"I hope I didn't chase him away," Ronald says as I return to check on the coffee.

"No, not at all," I say.

"You weren't taking my calls. I thought that maybe you were still angry with me."

"No, I'm not still angry. I was taking a vacation, that's all."

"Just to clear the air," Ronald says as I pour the coffee. "I was pretty mad with you, with what you said and everything…"

"I'm sorry about that, Ronald. There was so much going on up there…"

"But then I was glad. You were right to say those things and even though I got mad, I needed to hear them."

"Oh," I said, surprised. "There's cream in the fridge."

"I don't know how I'm sounding sometimes and if no one tells me... You were right to let me know, that's all."

"So, we're good?" I ask, making it sound like I'm ready to start work.

"Yeah, we're good."

As Ronald and I look over the changes to the stage design, I find it hard to get back into it and concentrate. I really wish that this whole project would go away and never come back but at the same time I have to appreciate having paid work to begin with: work is work.

"If there's something on your mind that maybe I could help you with, maybe I can return the favor?" Ronald asks.

"I'm sorry. I'm having a hard time with this," I admit.

"I've never asked about your personal life but I really don't mind hearing about it if you feel like talking to someone that cares and can maybe help?"

"Martin is twenty-four and after knowing me for like two weeks, just told me that he loved me," I said, encapsulating the situation as succinctly as I can.

"Wow," Ronald says. "That's pretty cool, huh?"

"No, it's not cool, Ronald. After two weeks, seriously?"

"Oh," he says, now seeing the problem. "You don't feel the same way?"

"It's too soon, obviously," I respond. "Isn't it?"

"I don't know, maybe. What's the recommended time frame for something like that, exactly?"

I look at Ronald trying to read whether he's being

serious or facetious but I can't tell. "Are you being serious?" I ask.

"Sure," he says. "I think it's beautiful for someone to declare their love and why shouldn't they announce it as soon as they know? It takes balls to say, 'I love you.' I've been seeing Frank for over two months now but I know that he's *never* going to say it to me. He's been hurt too many times. He'll probably never say it until he's on his deathbed or something."

"I don't think you quite know what I mean," I say, preferring not to say that our circumstances are not equal.

"Why, because it's different for gay couples?" he asks pointedly.

"No, not because you're gay. You two are around the same age, is what I meant."

"How long did it take your ex-husband to say that he loved you?"

"He told me on the first date," I answer and smile with the memory. When Ronald looks at me with total puzzlement, I feel like have to explain Bill a bit more to him so that he'll understand. "But that was so Bill," I say.

"He put it out there on the *first* date," Ronald said, like he was making a point and not asking a question.

"Yes, but that was Bill. He was ten years older; a man of the world. It wasn't like it was a big thing. He was trying to steal my heart but I was playing hard to get... I mean, I wasn't playing hard to get like I was leading him on; I was married at the time," I say but I stop because I'm not sure what point I'm making.

"It was all a game?" Ronald asks, trying also to see my point.

"No, I believe that he did love me from the beginning," I answer, now confused. "But he'd been around, so he knew what love was all about."

"And how did that work out for you?" he asks. By my expression, he could tell that I don't appreciate his flippancy.

"Okay," he says, his palms upturned in a gesture of surrender. "I don't have any wisdom to impart but what it sounds like to me is that you don't have a problem with the big 'I love you' being out there and whether it's too soon or not, is also irrelevant; what you do have a problem with is the age of the guy that's saying it."

"Maybe," I say, not that I necessarily agree but rather to end the discussion.

As I refocus my attention on the project, part of my brain is still thinking about Martin and age and love and experience. Am I unfairly discriminating against Martin because of his age? Am I saying that it's okay for an older guy to say 'I love you' on the first date but it's not okay for a younger guy to say it after two weeks? Is that what I really think?

If that is what I really think then I'm not giving Martin a fair chance. Again. Will I blame his age on everything he does that I don't agree with? Bill walked out on me a million times but I never once considered that he was acting immaturely; I just thought he was acting the way any guy would. Wow, I'm a closet ageist and I didn't even know it. If this is how *I* feel, what chance do we have when others act in an ageist way towards us as a couple?

"I think I do love Martin," I say to myself but when Ronald stops what he's doing and looks at me, I realize that I've said it out loud.

"Way to go," Ronald says and I'm sure he considered a high-five but stopped himself.

"I had this idea that because he's so young, he mustn't know anything about love," I say, smiling as a picture of his tender face comes floating into my mind's eye.

"Hey, I'm middle-aged and what the heck do I know about love?" Ronald asks.

"That's just it. It doesn't matter whether Martin knows anything about love; no one I know knows anything about love. What does matter is being open and willing to let love in, right?"

"There you go," Ronald says, like he's beginning to like his newly adopted role as my love coach. "I think you just hit the nail on the head."

As Ronald and I work more on the changes, I think of the fictional Therese. Her life is over yet she seems stuck in perpetual regret. When she was living, she engaged in a number of relationships with people but she moved on without resolving any of them. As soon as a problem arose, she would dump that relationship and move on to the next. Expecting the next relationship to be different, to her disappointment, she found it so similar to her previous relationships that she dumped that one, as well. And on and on she went, leaving half-fulfilled relationships littered in her wake. Then she died.

The play suggests that if Therese had her life to live over again, she would do things differently. Instead of shuffling from one unresolved relationship to the next, she would do her darned best to reach completion with each one. Only after all her best efforts had been exhausted, and she was out of solutions, would she consider that the relationship had run its course and she could move on to the next.

Have I reached a natural conclusion with Martin? No. If Therese was in my shoes, and the choice was put to her to choose either possible regret or possible love and happiness, what would she choose? Duh, don't have to be a genius to answer that one.

"So, hopefully this will satisfy them and finally put this project to bed, what do you say?" Ronald says, as he packs up to leave.

"I think I'll miss Therese," I say and I surprise myself by my sudden feelings of understanding and fondness for the play character.

"I thought you hated this project?"

"Did I say that?" I ask as I scan my memory banks for any such admission on my part (which I would consider unprofessional and just bad business practice).

"It's nothing that you've said, no; just the way you talk about it, I guess. Maybe I'm projecting. I don't like it, either."

"I didn't like it in the beginning but it did kinda grow on me," I say.

"Well, I'm out of here," Ronald says. "You do notice that I never mentioned Frank this whole time?" he asks, smiling.

"I did notice," I agree, even though he did mention him briefly. "I hope you do everything you can to work it out between you two and you don't end up in regret like Therese."

"Is that what the play is about?" Ronald asks and I'm not sure if he's joking or not. Ronald kisses me goodbye on the cheek and I decide not to ask any more questions for fear that he will stay longer.

When I close the front door behind Ronald, I turn and notice the state of the living room. There are hot embers smoldering in the fireplace; plates of half-eaten food dotted between the random collection of pillows on the floor; two glasses of red wine and an almost full bottle of wine. The memory of how I felt when I was enjoying all that makes me miss Martin and I almost fool myself by thinking that he's hanging out in the bedroom and is about to appear with a smile and a hug, any time now. I really want to see him and have him hold me till his arms get tired.

The thought of never seeing him again feels me with dread; did I chase him off for good, this time? Should I call him and apologize? Is he still angry with me and if I called him would he blow me off? Should I give him time to calm down and give him enough time for him to miss me? Yes. Should I finish my glass of wine rather than throwing it out? Yes, definitely.

As I put on some smooth jazz and sit by the fire with my glass of wine, I try to allow myself to really relax and apply my mom's maxim that, 'It is what it is.' There's no point in getting upset about something that may or may not happen I tell myself, as if I can hear my mother's voice explain her life philosophy to me.

I miss my mom. I miss her wisdom and her calming influence. What have I deprived myself of all these years living away from her and my sister? What kind of a different person would I have been had I stayed living up north? Has LA corrupted me? Have I really become an annoying, touchy-feely, LA speak, New Age idiot?

I didn't know that I feel all alone and adrift down here in La La land until my recent visit up north. Why now and not before? Did I always feel this way and never allowed myself to recognize it or am I feeling it now for the first time? Do I put too much of myself into a relationship with a man, as if that's the only relationship in my life that matters? Therese had unfulfilled relationships not just with lovers but also with family and to a lesser extent, friends and work colleagues.

When the doorbell rings I'm startled and I realize that I dozed off, empty wine glass in hand. When I open the door, Martin stands looking at me with the goofy, lost look on his face that always melts my heart. The radiance of the sun, glaring behind him, lights him from behind and makes it look like he has a halo. Before I give him a chance to open his mouth and totally ruin the moment, I engulf him in my arms and bury my face deep into his manly chest.

His body is tense and I know that he's waiting for me to break the embrace so that we can talk things out but I'm done talking and I don't let go; I hold him and I hold him and I hold him until his body gets the message that I'm not going to let go until he meets me where I am and not the other way around.

His body slowly relaxes and as I close the door with my foot, the darkness and privacy of the indoors helps his body to relax even more. It's the longest hug I've ever experienced with anybody and I still don't want it to end. As our energies merge, it feels like we are becoming one; we are no longer two separate beings trying to carve out and establish individual territories for ourselves; our territories overlap; there is no need to assert ourselves as competitors; we are on the same team.

I want to stay here where it's real and it's honest and it's dreamy and it's intoxicating.

"I'm so glad you came back," I tell him from a deep, strong and vulnerable place within me.

"Me too," he says, meeting me in that place.

"I love you too," I say and with the side of my face I can feel his heart restrict and then quickly expand, as if it just got a mild electric shock. A tear drops onto my cheek and I know that it didn't fall from either of my eyes.

I want to lie down and have him spoon me for the rest of eternity so I slowly tear myself from his chest and taking his hand in mine, I look into his eyes. "Come lie down and hold me," I say. His eyes are teary and preferring not to speak for fear that he may not be able to contain his tears, his head slightly nods, yes.

As he wraps me up in his arms on the bed, I tuck my body so totally into his that it feels like we are one person. My mind is so yielding and resplendent, I feel like we could be adrift either deep beneath the ocean or out yonder in the vastness of space. What I'm experiencing feels like the transcendent state I aspire to in my meditations but never quite attain. I feel not just one with Martin but one with the world; I am at one with the universe and all that is.

It is what it is.

I feel like I'm not just understanding it as a concept, I'm experiencing it with my entire being. As I'm conscious of surrendering further and further into the emptiness of space, my head feels heavier and heavier and the darkness becomes darker and darker... until I am, no more.

I must have turned over in my sleep; as I open my eyes, I'm directly facing Martin, who sleeps soundly. It feels like we've been napping for a few hours but I don't care to know how many exactly. I'm sure that Martin must have been a cute little kid; his face looks like a little toddler's face as he naps.

"Have you been watching me sleep?" he asks as he wakes.

"You're so well behaved when you sleep," I say, stroking his hair. I'm feeling soft and sexy and I'm hoping that he doesn't jump right up and ask what time it is that he needs to be someplace... and, thankfully, he doesn't. I'm also hoping that this time we can go real slow and that by seducing him, his inner puppy dog won't get triggered. I don't want him to morph from cool and sexy into his, 'Oh, yippee, all hands on deck, we're going to have sex,' persona.

As if approaching a possible explosive device, I move slowly and deliberately towards him and plant a very soft and tender kiss on his barely parted lips. I pull back to let him know that I'm now in control and he should stay exactly where he is as I very leisurely unbutton his shirt, button by ponderous button.

I can feel his body get aroused and the little smirk on his face that he tries to subdue is a dead giveaway that he knows what's coming. He's so excited, he can barely contain himself. If he was a little puppy, his tail would be seriously wagging right now. When I finally pop the last remaining button, I can feel him wanting to pounce but again, I warn him with my eyes not to dare move: this is my deal.

As I pull his shirt open I notice some major discoloration of the skin on his chest. I have to lean my head back to focus on what looks like a serious rash all over his front. "What's that?" I ask.

"What's what?" he replies and then he suddenly gets nervous.

"It looks like you have some kind of rash on your chest."

"Oh, that, no, it's not a rash," he says, acting guilty. "I was going to tell you..."

"Tell me what?" I ask, major alarm bells going off in my head.

"I dropped by Janice's place on my way home."

"Janice lives in Venice? That's not on your way home?"

"I wanted to return her DVD which was in my bag all the time and I...she told me to take care of it for her, that night, and I forgot and I figured she needed it and I was going to Venice anyway, to take some photos for a project I'm working on and anyway..."

I'm up and out of the bed standing with my feet on the floor before I even became aware that I had decided to get up.

"Nothing happened," Martin says as he gets out of the bed to come to me. He keeps talking but I don't hear him and the last thing I want is for him to touch me... so I bolt to the kitchen.

"I don't want to hear any more," I say as he comes and stops in the kitchen doorway. "You should leave."

"I don't want to leave," he says and his blank refusal surprises me. "I want to talk this out."

"There is really nothing to talk about, Martin. Please go."

"Frances, nothing happened between us. Can't we even discuss it?"

I'm done talking with Martin and I can barely even look in his direction. I feel positively ill. I can't even allow my mind to delve deeply into what is happening. I can't let my imagination start to create images that involve both my daughter and this young man. I take a deep breath. If I ignore him and continue to make some coffee, I expect him to get the message and clear out and leave me the heck alone. Martin doesn't leave. I don't want to look at him but beyond thinking that he's an imbecile, I've no idea why he's still standing there.

"Frances," he finally says in a soft and measured tone like the tone that someone might use to address a person standing out on a ledge of a tall building. "If I have learned anything from you it's that honest communication is paramount to having any kind of relationship, with anybody. I know you feel like you hate me or despise me at this moment and I can understand that but if I walk out that door, then there's probably no way we can come back from this. You said you wanted a conscious relationship with true and honest communication? Well, here it is. Or do you only want it when it's on your terms?"

"You crossed a line, Martin," I say, not at all

appreciating his patronizing tone.

"Can you stop doing what you're doing and we can sit down and talk?"

"Fine," I say, as I put down the dish cloth. "Let's talk."

CHAPTER 16

Martin sits me down on the sofa and I take a few deliberate deep breaths to calm down as I remind myself not to jump to conclusions and be open and unbiased to what he has to say.

"I was kinda angry when I left here earlier," he says. I don't face him but instead sit at the far end of the sofa and stare straight ahead, as if to say, "I'm listening."

"When I threw my bag into the car, Janice's DVD came flying out and I remembered that she asked me to look after it for her and give it to her when I was done watching it. It wasn't very good," he says, smiling to break the mood, "but don't tell her I said that."

I don't respond so he gets the message that he should get on with it.

"Her address is on the case so I figured that she needed it and that I'd swing by on my way home. I know it's not exactly on my way home but I was upset and I didn't particularly want to go home... I thought maybe being at the beach would be nice and I could take some photos of the beach freaks... anyway," he pauses and I can feel him wanting me to chill out and tell him that everything's okay.

"So you went to the address," I say, prompting him to continue.

"Yeah, she lives in this, like, beach commune with all these hippie kids. So she's happy to get her DVD back and she introduces me to her roommate, Jane, the actress from the video."

As soon as Martin mentions Janice's girlfriend, I begin to relax more. Janice is into girls and no way would she be into someone like Martin. The fact that Janice was with her girlfriend when Martin came along suggests that maybe Janice was making fun of Martin from the very beginning. When she met him and hung out with him, she didn't even tell him that she was my daughter; what was that all about?

"So she gives me a beer and tells me that I would look amazing with one of her henna tattoos. I've never had a tattoo and she says that these ones wash off; so I said, what the heck, let's go for it. I picked out one of her Celtic designs and she says, "great choice, take off your shirt; this one goes on the chest." So, I take my shirt off and I'm thinking that this is going to look really cool. Except, when she's finished and I take a look at it…"

Martin opens up his shirt to show me Janice's handiwork. On his chest is written two, crudely drawn words: Hello Mom.

"I honestly don't know if she was protecting you from another sex-crazed boyfriend or trying to get one over on you by bragging that she could have stolen a boyfriend from you, I don't know."

"Could she?" I ask. "Could she have stolen a boyfriend from me?"

"Of course not," Martin says as if I just suggested the most ridiculous thing he's ever heard. I'm shocked and appalled by Janice's behavior and I've no idea if this latest stunt of hers is intended as a joke or if she's out to hurt me or punish me in some way. "She is going through some weird phase, lately," I say to Martin, turning my body more fully towards him.

"How do you mean?"

"All this feminist stuff, she was never like that before. It's probably a mix of whatever feminist courses she's doing in college and a belated adolescence where she seems to blame me for all her childhood instability, not having a father… She actually told me that I ruined her entire childhood," I say, which was much harder to admit than I thought it would be. Thankfully, Martin gets the sense to hold me while my tears come and as I melt back into his arms again, I wonder to myself just how much more heartache I can truly withstand.

Even though I had a good cry, my senses remain numb for the rest of the evening. I'm done with talking and analyzing and if Martin or anyone were to ask, "How are you feeling?" I truly feel like I might stab them in the chest.

For supper, Martin and I finish off the Chinese food while watching some dumb movie on cable. I don't particularly want Martin to be here but at the same time, I don't want him to leave me alone. If I was left here, all by myself, I don't doubt that I could spiral down into an even deeper level of despair than the one I can't seem to get out of, right now.

I wake up the next morning not feeling much better than the night before, in fact, it's as if I never slept at all; I don't feel at all rested. Martin stayed over but neither of us seemed to be in the mood for anything except sleep. "We should get ready for the seminar," I say to him when we both wake.

"You still want to go?" he asks.

"You don't?"

"No, I do. I wasn't sure if… Sure, let's go," he says.

I don't particularly want to go out or do anything, for that matter; but I feel like if I don't have anything to do to fill up my time, I'll just mope around the apartment and isolate, which is clearly not healthy. I know that I need to have a showdown with Janice and find out what her deal is but I don't have the strength for that today. I really should have reached out to her sooner and insisted that we meet up and talk things through. The longer I've allowed her resentment to build the worse her behavior towards me has become.

The seminar is being held in a small function room of a downtown hotel and when we get there, I'm beginning to regret it, already. Eager and adoring couples are everywhere and the way that some of them look at each other, with practically stars in their eyes... it makes me want to throw up.

I'm so not in the mood to be a witness to public displays of affection by couples who seem to think that if they attend a couples' seminar, they are somehow putting themselves at an advantage to the rest of us. They all look like they have an air of smug superiority about them and there's no way I could imagine my sister lasting more than two seconds among them.

The first topic on the agenda concerns the biological and evolutionary foundations to mate selection and when I see a bullet list on the blackboard of topics, I know exactly where they are going to go with this. I'm familiar with the biological argument that guys argue in defense of their promiscuity. They like to think that their evolutionary biology, which has hardwired their brains, gives them a free pass to desire and/or screw any woman that arouses them sexually, which, as far as I can tell, is just about any woman that's willing.

"The concern of evolution is not that you have someone to go to the movies with or to ensure that you have a dance partner, no," some geeky-looking guy in a white lab coat says as he continues his PowerPoint presentation. "The concern of evolution is the continuance of the species. It's the evolutionary impulse that is largely responsible for mate selection among animals. Humans, despite whether we might like to think otherwise, are no exception to that impulse."

Martin turns to me, with a smirk on his face, as if he hopes to recruit me to be his heckling buddy. He obviously doesn't see how serious the implications of all this pseudo science are, so I only politely acknowledge him.

"In the absence of social restrictions, the human male would be promiscuous throughout the whole of his life. Women, however, tend to be more monogamous. Women want a lot of sex with the man they love; men want to have a lot of sex with a lot of different women," the "doctor" continues.

To make his point, he actually shows a video of a pair of rats in a cage... copulating. After a while, they stop and the good doctor tells us that they have become bored with each other. However, when the female rat is replaced by a different female rat, the male becomes interested in sex again and away they go, copulating like crazy.

"Scientists have called this the Columbus Effect. The same behavior is observed with monkeys and yes, you guessed it, humans. Sexual boredom is one of the strongest factors operating against stable relationships in both the human and animal kingdom. When sex between a man and woman in relationship comes to a halt... a break up in the relationship is sure to follow."

I hear Martin sniggering and he's probably wondering why I don't find the whole thing hilarious. I don't find it hilarious because it means that if all this scientific mumbo-jumbo is true, then men and women don't stand a chance to have a long-lasting romantic relationship. If this is even only slightly true, then it means that evolution has stacked the deck and the joke is on us humans.

If women are only expected to be carriers of children and all men want to do is "procreate" with as many women as they possibly can… then I want no part of it. Giving birth to Janice, I've already performed my role for the future and betterment of humanity so what's in it for me? Am I to be cast onto the trash heap of useless humanity?

As I look at the two rats copulating — the female looks like she's not even enjoying it — I can see the face of Bill superimposed on the head of the male rat. The 'Columbus Effect' (Columbus discovered the New World, get it?) describes him exactly, as a matter of fact. He screwed me senseless for a few years until boredom and familiarity set in and he lost interest. When some fresh new vagina came along, he left me to screw that and he's probably on to rat number four at this point in time.

The whole thing just makes me sick to my stomach; all I can see in front of me is sex and all I can hear repeating over and over in my head is the word sex, sex, sex, sex…

I'm on my feet and out the door before I'm aware that I'd made a decision to leave.

"Frances," Martin calls out and catches up to me as I leave the building.

"I can't do this," I tell him.

"Me neither," he says. "That thing sucked."

"I mean I can't this… I can't do us. I'm sorry."

"That's it?" he asks looking crestfallen. "After all the talk about issues and honest communication and stuff? You're just going to walk?"

"I can't do this anymore," I say and turn to go.

"Frances," he calls and once again catches up to me. Taking my hands in his, he looks soulfully into my eyes. "Frances, you're a beautiful, caring, wonderful woman and…"

I wait for him to finish his sentence but he seems to have forgotten what he was about to say. When I move to walk, he clenches my hands tighter, as if he just remembered. "I'm really sorry you can't follow your own advice," he finally says.

I don't know how to respond to that so I let go of his hands and walk. What I should have told him is that men and women are just not meant to be together in the way that I want us to be together. We are hard-wired to want different things in relationship and they are not at all compatible. I want Zen; men want sex.

Most consider anger to be a negative emotion, and it probably is, but over the next few days I kinda enjoy hanging out in it. It seems to act as an antidote to my depression and I'm actually getting a lot done. Not only do I do weeks of built up laundry, I also give the apartment a much deserved, thorough cleaning.

I call Janice a few times but each time she fails to take my call because she's most likely well aware that I'm going to rip her a new one. On my final attempt, I leave her a voicemail message: "Janice, this is your mom again. We need to talk and you're not going to put me off forever. You're going to meet me for lunch at my place on Sunday at noon. You don't have school and I don't care what else you've got going on, you will show up hungry and on time. I'm not inviting you; I'm telling you."

I also call Ronald and ask him to send me some work, any work, and he promises me that he will. He tells me that he and Frank are still trying to work things out.

I call and talk to my mom for the longest time and soon after I have an equally long and pleasant talk with my sister. Despite giving her lots of opportunity, she still doesn't confide in me or share anything significant of her life. I do tell them that I miss them both and that we should talk much more often than we normally do. It's a desire I'm going to do my best to keep up. I miss them both so much.

I also do lots of thinking about my life and strange as it may sound, I actually do a lot of thinking even when I'm not aware that I am thinking; it's as if even though I'm watching TV or leafing through a magazine or whatever, there's a lot of thinking going on in some other part of my brain. Now and again (most usually when I wake in the morning), I might get an idea 'from nowhere' or just maybe an update.

A lot of times, when I'm talking to someone, for instance, I'll announce the decisions or the results of such subconscious thinking processes, which is oftentimes as new to my ears as it is to theirs. Like when I go to my next session with Dr. Roberts, for example.

"This is going to be my last session," I inform her as soon as our preliminary pleasantries are exchanged. I know that she's shocked by my declaration but she's trying not to show it.

"May I ask why?" she asks.

"I've decided to make some changes in my life," I say. "I'm moving back up north to be closer to my mom and my sister."

"I don't remember you mentioning that," she says and I can see that she's finding it harder to disguise her surprise. "Is this a sudden decision?"

"Yes, as a matter of fact. I don't know what I'm doing here in LA anymore. I want my sister back. I want my mom."

"You want your mommy?" Dr. Roberts asks and she says it so quickly that I'm wondering if she had really intended it to sound as condescending as I heard it. Being the professional, however, I know that she's going to maintain a stoic look on her face and even if she was being inappropriate, she's going to wait and see what my response will be. I decide to ignore it altogether.

"I want my family back," I say.

"When will you be moving?"

"I don't know, probably not for a while. I have to figure out a way to make it happen."

"But you're ending your sessions as of now?"

"Yes."

Dr. Roberts sits back in her chair and I know that's an indication that she now expects me to do all the talking. "These sessions have been terrific and I've learnt so much about myself over the years. You've been extremely helpful and quite honestly, I don't know what I would have done without them, without you being here for me. I can't thank you enough but I really think that it's time for me to move on."

"Explain what you mean by moving on?"

I take a breath and sigh and in an effort to gather my thoughts, I turn to look out of her window. I don't have it all worked out and much of what I'm saying now is the accumulation of thoughts that I have been thinking since my recent trip up north; actually, they started before that when I went to the pub and had that crazy night with Martin.

"I need to take charge of my life again. I don't know when precisely I lost control and pinpointing it to any one moment or several moments isn't important right now. What is important is that I stop seeing myself as a victim; as someone that things happen to, as if I have no control over what happens to me. I need to stand up for myself and tell people where to get off; to call them on their shit and not accept how they behave towards me, if it hurts me in any way, for instance."

"Is it true that you have been playing a victim, Frances?" Dr. Roberts asks as if I need to look at that more fully.

"I don't know if playing the victim is the right term; I'm sure you hear it a lot; it's become a cliché and there's a load of self-help books written about it; I know because I've read my share..." I say and pause when I feel like I'm losing my way.

"You can learn a lot about yourself by the way that people in your life see you, right?" I continue. "I see myself in a certain way but it's not the same way that others see me; there's a disconnect; and I know that, maybe 90 percent of the time, that disconnect is because I've been deceiving myself: the person I see myself as being... is not the person I really am."

"Can you explain that?"

"In my head, I see myself as a strong, independent, capable and compassionate human being. That's not how others see me."

"How do others see you?"

"Okay... Bill saw me as someone compliant who maybe disagreed with him slightly now and then but would ultimately always agree with him and do what he wanted, even if it was against her own wishes or life philosophy. Steve sees me like I'm a small bird with a broken wing. Janice thinks that I'm a narcissistic crazy person and doesn't respect me in the slightest. My mom pities me as being someone that's emotionally delicate and ineffective in life and my sister thinks overall, that I'm an idiot. She doesn't even feel like she can trust me or confide in me with some serious issues that she's going through."

"That's very astute of you to look at that. Has the 'new' you given up on relationship, as well?"

"I've given up on thinking that I can have a certain type of relationship. I've been doing relationship the wrong way around."

"Explain that?"

"I had an image in my head of what relationship should be and then I'd try to fit the person into that model. I think it should be the other way around. I need to see and accept the person for who he is and then fit the relationship into the best fit for him and me together."

"You're experiencing some wonderful growth, Frances. Can you talk more about that?"

"I walked out of a relationship seminar when they were explaining the biological underpinnings of human mating. What I heard them say was that men are designed by evolution as some kind of indiscriminate sperm disseminator and women are designed to be a sperm receptor and infant incubator, period."

"A pretty crude way of putting it," Dr. Roberts says, looking amused.

"They pretty much said that when a man and a woman get together sexually, each of their bodies produce chemicals and hormones to give them each a feeling of euphoria so that they will stay with each other long enough to produce offspring."

"Which we interpret as, 'falling in love.'"

"The body gradually stops producing these hormones and chemicals for, I think, seven years, after which nature assumes that the offspring are old enough that they don't need a male parent anymore and maybe the male goes off to produce more offspring with another female."

"You've heard of the seven year itch, right? Nature is very clever, you must admit." Dr. Roberts says, clearly enjoying this session.

"I wanted to think that it was bull crap because that doesn't jibe with the image of men and romantic relationship in my head. But then again, it is what it is, right? We are spiritual beings inhabiting animal bodies so of course we'd have biological underpinnings. But we're not victims of evolution or maybe I should say that we don't have to be simple biological... zombies that are slaves to our biology."

"Correct."

"When I have an urge to have a baby, for instance, which I don't, I can take into consideration the fact that there are hormones being released in my body to prompt me in that direction. When I'm 'falling in love' I can recognize that part of the reason I'm feeling that way is because certain hormones are being released into the blood stream..." I say and pause because I feel like I'm rambling and I've lost my point.

"So, having this understanding of the part that nature and our bodies play in romance is another piece for you to consider in the decision-making process," Dr. Roberts says helpfully.

"That's right. It also helps me understand men a bit more. I've no idea what goes on in their heads but a large part of their behavior is being influenced by very similar biological impulses."

"Well, seems like you're getting a handle on things," Dr. Roberts says as I relax more and she senses that I'm winding down on my mind dump.

"Yeah," I agree, feeling proud of myself. "It certainly does."

"That's terrific, Frances but I hope that you realize that these are not new concepts; in fact, we've talked a lot along these lines over the years. Perhaps these truths are only now sifting down into your consciousness in order for you to fully embody them and take them on board, so to speak?"

"I think that I've understood things mentally but they existed more as neat ideas rather than a real living philosophy that I was integrating into my actual life and affairs."

"Well, I greatly encourage this new attitude; it really sounds like you're ready to take the bull by the horns and fully participate in life as a player, rather than as a bystander. You know that I'll always be here for you."

"Yes, thank you. As I say, these sessions have been immensely helpful to me. Whenever I'm faced with a decision or a quandary, I ask myself, 'what would Dr. Roberts' say?' Your advice helps me even when I'm not here."

"That's very good to hear, Frances. Thank you."

"Thank you."

I know that I'm going to miss my therapy sessions with Dr. Roberts and it is with some trepidation that I discontinue. However, I also feel that I may have been using our sessions together as something of a crutch and an excuse for me to stay more focused on the past than on my future. I know that I can always return to therapy if I need to and I'm definitely not unhappy about the money that I'm going to save by not coming to see her.

I'll need all the funds I can muster if I truly am going to move up north. I haven't at all worked out any details and at this point it is more of a dream than a reality. Real estate is at a premium where I'd wish to live and although I still have some funds in the bank leftover from the divorce, it's nowhere near the amount I'd need to buy a house. I'm sure I could stay with my mom temporarily but I'd prefer if that suggestion came from her and not from me.

Work will be a problem. I may still be able to work the odd project for Ronald but, considering his client base is mainly focused in the entertainment industry in LA, I won't be able to count on it. I could fall back on my interior design work but I'd be so rusty and so far behind in design trends that I may not be able to compete effectively in such a crowded market place. Let's just see how it goes, I guess.

CHAPTER 17

When I wake up on Sunday morning and turn on my laptop, a calendar reminder pops up to tell me that today is the day of the wedding. It takes me a few seconds to remember my promise to Martin that I would accompany him to his ex-girlfriend's marriage, no matter what.

I didn't hear back from Janice to confirm and as I prepare lunch I put aside any doubts that I have that she won't show up. If she shows, she shows I tell myself. If not, not. No biggie.

When she does arrive, on time and telling me that she's famished, I give her a warm hug and welcome. I'm delighted to see her and I'm going to put my foot down that we see each other much more often than we do. We see each other so rarely, it's not even funny. I give her a drink and tell her to sit down as I lay out the food on the coffee table.

"You're not in trouble," I say to her as she sheepishly sits across from me on the sofa. "I *was* angry with you but I'm not anymore. You probably even did me a favor. You gave me the kick in the pants I obviously needed to make some changes in my life."

The tension on Janice's face relaxes but she still stays quiet, probably deciding to adopt a wait and see approach.

"We're going to do this every week," I tell her. "I don't care what's going on in your life or what deadlines you've got for school... you'll have to work your schedule around it. We're meeting here for lunch every Sunday, okay?"

Janice looks at me like it's not okay and I've just added yet another chore for her to grit her teeth while doing but, still, she stays quiet.

"If you get tired driving up here all the time, then maybe we can meet half-way at a café someplace, alright?"

"Whatever," Janice finally says.

"Is there something that you want to tell me?" I ask.

"No," she answers.

"There's nothing on your mind; maybe something you want to say to me to get off your chest? Now's a good time."

"No," Janice says like it's an out-there suggestion.

"Do you want to tell me why you're so angry with me, then?"

"I'm not angry."

"Maybe a little passive-aggressive, maybe?"

"Look, that whole thing with Martin... I was just having fun; making a joke, that's all," she says dismissively.

"Which part of that was funny, Janice?" I ask in an unthreatening voice.

"I was just... Martin is such a Dorkool, that's all."

"Martin is a what?" I ask, not familiar with the term.

"He's a Dorkool. A dork that thinks he's cool," Janice answers, smiling.

"So, you wanted to show him up or something?" I ask, trying to understand.

"I don't know, I guess. I wanted you to see him for who he is. It was funnier in my head... when I did it, I'm sorry."

"You wanted me to see him as he really is: a dork that's trying to be cool?" I ask, hoping to get it right.

"Yeah."

"You don't think I see him as a dork?"

"Obviously not."

"So, what, you were trying to protect me from the scary clutches of dorks or something?"

"I told you... it was funnier in my head. I didn't think it would go this far. I didn't think you'd break up with the guy."

"I didn't break up with him because of you, Janice and I didn't break up with him because he's a dork trying to be cool. That's the best part of him, if you must know."

"Since when did you start liking dorks?" Janice asks, unable to contain her giggling.

"Janice, why don't you just admit that you're angry with me and a large part of your stunt was to hurt me? Because it did hurt, Janice. And I don't believe that you were trying to protect me... you were trying to hurt me, admit it."

"Do we have to do this, mom?" Janice asks in the way she has of seeking my sympathy.

"Yes, sweetie. We do."

Janice takes a sip of her coffee and looking around the room, visibly pouts.

"What did you mean when you said that I had ruined your life?"

Janice looks at me like that she couldn't believe I was bringing that up. "Seriously, mom? I was angry. I said stuff I didn't mean. Like we all do."

"You *don't* believe that I ruined your childhood?"

"Mom, I'm bored already. Do we really have to do this?"

"If not now, when, Janice?"

"Mom, I'm sorry I hurt you and I'm real sorry that I said stuff when I was angry..." she says, trying but not succeeding in sounding sincere. "I'm really sorry."

Taking her hands into mine I lean forward and look her meaningfully in the eyes. "I'm the one that's sorry," I say. "It can't have been easy for you not knowing who your real father is. It can't have been easy for you losing the only dad you did get to know. We never really discussed all that, when Bill left. I was just too... too much in my own pain to pay you the kind of consideration and attention that you should have been getting from me, your mother. Janice, I really am sorry."

"It's okay, mom," Janice says, as if she's more uncomfortable with me embarrassing her than having hurtful emotions of her own.

"It's okay if you blame me," I continue. "It's okay if you hate me, even. It's perfectly understandable if you do. It's perfectly understandable if you really feel that I ruined your life."

"I don't feel that way, Mom," she says, and I sense that she's not fully connecting with her emotions. "It's just that..." Janice hesitates and looks away.

"Tell me, sweet pea. It's just that, what?"

"It's just that you've always given me the impression that I was the one that ruined *your* life."

Not at all expecting to hear such a pronouncement from my daughter, I can feel my entire body freeze, as though in shock.

"It's not that you've ever said anything," Janice continues. "But I've always gotten the impression that if you didn't have me... if you didn't get pregnant back then... that your life would have been different, would have been better. I know that you love me and everything, it's not that... I just never felt like you really wanted me, I guess, like I was a mistake, your one big, big mistake."

When Janice sees that I'm not moving and yet tears are streaming down my face, she gets worried. "Oh, mom, I don't mean it. I don't hate you," she says, pulling me up towards her so that she can hug me and maybe assist my body to thaw out and start moving again. "You feel so cold," she says.

"I do feel cold," I say and I can feel her relief that I actually spoke.

"Will I go get a blanket?" she asks.

"Maybe in a minute," I answer. "For now, just hold me."

Janice holds me tight and rocks me in her arms as I hold her in return and without either of us wishing to speak, we silently proclaim and exchange the deep love that we share for each other. We hold each other for what seems like a long time and as my body temperature returns to normal, I kiss her head and whisper into her ear. "You didn't ruin my life, you *saved* my life. I wasn't expecting you but you're the best thing that ever happened to me. Truly."

Janice quickly rubs my arm with her hand as if signaling that she appreciates the sentiment but she also wishes to break from her embrace. As if we were both so emotionally overwrought from our sharing, we both instinctively know that neither of us is in any state or frame of mind to continue at such an emotionally raw level.

"This was a good start," I say, as if I'm acknowledging that we're done with the heavy stuff, for now.

"To be continued," Janice says, smiling and sighing with relief. "We should eat something, huh? I think the coffee has gone cold."

"I'll make a new pot," I say, cheering up. "I don't know about you but I'm famished."

"Totally," she concurs.

Janice and I talk about all kinds of things as I make a fresh pot of coffee and we finally get to dig in and eat our fill of cheeses, fruits and pastries. She tells me all about her life at school and how pretentious she finds most of the other students. She's not sure if a life in Hollywood would at all suit her but she does light up with passion when she talks about film and expresses an interest in making documentaries.

I admit to her of my jealousy regarding her relationship with my family that I know nothing about and that she seems to confide in them more than she does her own mother.

"They never judge me, mom. They accept me, as I am," she explains.

"I don't judge you, sweetie," I protest. "I accept you."

"No, you don't, mom but that's okay," she says, smiling. "You're my mom. I expect you to have opinions about what I'm doing with my life. If you didn't care, I wouldn't feel loved by you, would I?"

"I guess not. I try not to judge," I say.

"You're doing fine, mom. I'm looking forward to our weekly Sunday brunches already."

"You are?" I ask, a broad smile breaking out on my face.

"Aren't you?" she asks, also smiling.

"More than you know," I say. "What are you doing later on?" I ask, as I check the time.

"I'm going to a screening with Jane but that's not for a few hours, why?"

"How would you like to help pick out something for me to wear to a wedding?"

"You're going to a wedding?" she asks. "Today?"

"I wasn't sure I was going to go... until now. I don't have much time."

"Who's getting married?"

"Martin's ex-girlfriend."

Janice looks at me with a priceless, puzzled facial

expression that I wish I had my smart phone handy so I could take a picture. "You do know that Martin is a big goofball, right?" she asks.

"Yeah," I answer, smiling. "I know." When Janice makes a face as if to say, 'whatever,' I add with a cheesy grin, "Hey, the heart wants... what the heart wants."

I've been playing angry chick music all week and as I drive to the wedding on this beautiful sunny day, it still remains my music of choice.

I run through various scenarios in my head which run the gamut from Martin not showing up to Martin showing up with someone else or Martin showing up but not wanting to see me. Such thoughts of possible eventualities would have paralyzed the old me into staying at home but the new me sweeps all concerns aside with the simple maxim: it is what it is. In other words, I'll deal with whatever faces me when it faces me and not before.

Luckily the church is in Brentwood, which is but a stone's throw from my apartment. If it doesn't work out, I can take a drive up the coast and maybe have supper in Santa Barbara or somewhere equally nice. Maybe take a ramble up State Street, do some window shopping and possibly take a sunset stroll along the beach. It's all good.

Finding parking is a little tricky. As I enter the charming little chapel I find that most attendees are more concerned with what they're wearing and how they look than they are about wondering who belongs and who does not. I scan every row from the front to the rear, where I sit, but I don't see any sign of Martin.

Despite her obvious nervousness, the bride looks amazing dressed in what I'm pretty certain is a Vera Wang wedding dress. The groom seems equally nervous but he also looks at his bride like he can't believe his luck, which is very cute and adorable. The service is short and sweet and as everyone makes their way out of the chapel, I stay in my seat and, in case I've missed him, I watch for Martin, who, by now I sadly must conclude is a no-show.

I'm more disappointed than I expected I would be and now I feel like I *have* to see his goofy, smiley, soft and tender face or I'll never experience a moment of happiness again. I feel like asking one of the guys if they know him but I doubt if Martin is known by anyone here, considering that she is his ex. Did I totally blow it with Martin? Did I treat him unfairly and blame him for my perceived failings of his sex, in general?

I don't get the sense that he has met someone else and I suspect that if he didn't attend the service, he's not going to show up at the reception all by himself, either. The reception is right across the street and I feel like I shouldn't give up on him, just yet. Perhaps because it's a joyous occasion, I find that most people smile back at me when I smile at them and everybody appears to be especially friendly.

A live band plays some really nice, jazzy music and as I watch them perform, I remind myself that I should get out more and listen to live music. I feel oddly comfortable mixing and mingling among the revelers who are strangers and in some ways I feel happily invisible. It's as if I'm in one of those dreams where you're in a scene among people that greet you kindly but there's no real interaction. It feels so good to be out of the house.

It does not feel good, however, to be missing Martin so much. I so wish he was here and we could dance and laugh and goof around together. He's such a fun partner and I laugh so much when I'm with him. I don't remember having as much fun with someone, male or female, than when I'm with Martin. Talk about bringing out your inner kid.

After a couple of hours that felt like a few minutes, I decide to have one more drink before I call it a day. Whatever concoction they mixed into the punch bowl is refreshing and delicious, so I help myself to another full glass. When I turn back around, I get the surprise of my life. I've only seen it in movies where you see someone among a crowd and yet your vision becomes so focused on them, it's as if the crowd parts and they become the focus, even though they aren't really.

Whatever effect that is... it's happening to me. Martin stands still and with a puzzled and captivated expression, he watches me back. I've never been so delighted to see anyone in my life. "Frances?" he asks, as if he's half-deciding to pinch himself. "What are you doing here?"

"I thought you were a no-show," I say, trying to tone down my inner glee.

"What? No, I mean, we missed the ceremony but...what are *you* doing here?" he asks, still looking terribly confused.

"*We* missed the ceremony?" I ask, my heart having skipped a beat on the 'we.' "Did you bring somebody?"

"Yeah. I brought my roommate, Mike. The sorry looking dude sitting by himself over by the kid's table," he says and in that moment I'm positive that everyone milling around can feel the sudden release of tension, previously emanating from my body, which just left the room.

"He's not looking too good," I say as I see a really cute guy who looks either very drunk or very hung-over.

"His girlfriend broke up with him and I guess he's experiencing PEA withdrawal," Martin says, referring to the hormonal-chemical soup that the body makes when a person is feeling "in love." Thoughts of that horrible couple's seminar flash briefly through my mind.

"What about you?" I ask. "Any PEA withdrawal symptoms you'd like to share?"

"Maybe later. What I would like to know is what you're doing here. Not that I'm not pleased to see you, I am. Very much so."

"I'm here because you invited me. I said, yes, that no matter what happens with us, I will go with you, remember? I may be a scaredy cat when it comes to relationships, but when it comes to attending other people's weddings... I'm pretty much good to my word."

"Are you alone?" Martin asks, his eyes darting quickly behind me.

"Of course. I almost went home after the ceremony but I decided, what the heck, maybe I'll meet someone special at the reception," I say playfully. "And I was right."

"What now?" he asks nervously.

"Well, I think we should stick to the plan, don't you?"

"What plan?"

"We dance and cavort and frolic in front of the bride and all of the time I won't be able to keep my roving hands off of you."

"That sounds like a good plan to me," he says as I see his entire body finally relax and a genuine smile light up his face.

"Showing up with sadsack over there... she already thinks you're a loser, right?" I say, winding him up.

"Oh, yeah," he says as he gives a wave to clueless Mike.

"We'll show her, then," I say as I take his hand and lead him to the dance floor. I can't honestly remember the last time I was out on a dance floor but I've obviously forgotten how much fun dancing is; or should I say, how much fun dancing with the right partner is. Martin is one of those dancers that make a lot of facial expressions along with making his moves. I'm pretty sure that Martin and guys like him never practiced their moves in front of a mirror and you have to give them credit for being so out there, regardless of how geeky they look on the dance floor.

Martin looks so downright dorky at times that I'm not sure if he's being serious or making fun but, either way, unlike a whole bunch of other dancers who stare at him with perhaps the same question in their heads, I don't care. Who says you have to look cool all the time? I follow along with Martin as best as I can and dare myself to be as courageous by also leaving my inhibitions behind. I'm sure that I too look like the Queen of the Dorks (or is it, Dorkools?), but I don't give a darn.

We dance till the last note of the live band is played and when they turn the music over to a manic live DJ who definitely is trying too hard to sound and look cool, we call it an evening. When we get back to my place in what seems like the blink of an eye, we engage in what I consider to be the grossest cliché of movie romance: the I-can't-wait-to-rip-those-clothes-off-you-and-get-you-into-bed maneuver. I soon discover that what looks annoying as all get out in a movie, it's actually a ton of fun in practice.

When we do finally get to my bed, I slow things right down by grabbing his shoulders and holding him at arms' length. I want this to last, I tell him with my eyes and as if he understood me perfectly, he smiles and begins stroking my neck and shoulders with his finger tips. Ooh... who would have thought that non-sexual contact could be such a turn on? My flesh breaks out in goose bumps and I'm beginning to think that if he could keep this up, he could give me my first big O. Definitely something to consider for our future together.

When Martin leaves the next morning to go do a job, I'm aware that I have mixed feelings. I'm sad that he's leaving but I'm also a bit pleased that we don't have the opportunity of spending too much intense time together, too soon. The enforced break between us gives me a chance to catch my breath and prevents me from losing myself totally into Martin's gravitational orbit. We have lots of time and there's no point in rushing or forcing things. Not that things feel in any way forced; quite the opposite. This is one of the most effortless and laid back relationships I've ever been involved with.

As I'm putting on some coffee, my phone rings and my heart sinks a little that it's not playing, '*Good Vibrations*.'

"Hello?" I answer.

"Frances. It's Jonathan."

"Who?" I ask before I suddenly recognize the name and voice.

"Jonathan from café Luna. Don't hang up," he says quickly. "I know it's been a while but I'm calling to apologize and I didn't think that you'd take my call before now."

"Jonathan, you've really nothing to apologize for," I say, anxious to get off the phone.

"But I do," he insists. "I acted really badly."

"Don't worry about it," I say dismissively. "I really have to go."

"Just give me a minute to explain," he says.

"I really don't have time, Jonathan," I say, just as the doorbell rings. "I've got someone at my front door, I really have to go. I accept your apology," I say as I hang up.

When I open the front door, Jonathan stands smiling, yet still managing to look sheepish. He carries a bunch of red roses and a large box of chocolates in his hands.

"Please just give me two minutes to explain," he says pleadingly. "Then I'll get out of your hair, for good."

"How did you know where I lived?" I ask, feeling a bit spooked.

"This is the mailing address on your business card," he answers, a little baffled. "Give me two minutes to explain myself."

"You have two minutes," I say as I let him in.

As I direct him to sit down, I purposely don't offer him coffee even though the aroma of a freshly brewed pot wafts agreeably through the apartment.

"I know that you must think of me as some kind of player, who doesn't take you very seriously, but I want you to know that that's not true. I take you very seriously," Jonathan begins.

"Look, there's really no..."

"Please, let me finish," he interrupts and I decide to just let him say his piece and be done with it.

"I liked you from the first moment I saw you. I knew right away that we'd have a connection; it's like I knew you already... and that you knew me, like you could *see* me... and I know that you did."

I'm not sure if he's expecting me to agree or deny at this point but I don't give anything away and instead stay silent with my eyes looking down, as if I expect him to say what he needs to say and leave.

"After the first night I saw you, I asked Stephanie — the hostess — that if you ever came in again when I was on my shift, to seat you in my section, which thankfully, she did."

That explains the same seat, every time, I almost say out loud.

"When I asked you out for coffee, and you accepted, I was over the moon... but when you wanted to leave so early, I *knew* that you weren't thinking of seeing me again and if I was going to have a chance with you, I needed to make it count, then and there. The thing about the painting is only partly a lie. You see, you do remind me of someone else, someone I was so desperately in love with and seeing you seemed to wake something up inside of me; something that I had thought had gone to sleep. You made me want to paint again. After all these years — you must understand that I thought that I would never ever paint again — but just seeing your beautiful face made me want to take up my brush and paint you."

I resist the urge to look up and risk meeting my eyes with his but I get the impression from the quiver in his voice that his eyes are teary and with any kind of encouragement from me, this peculiar interlude has the possibility of going horribly wrong. Jonathan stands and I look up at him but then quickly focus my eyes on the Monet print on the wall behind him.

"So, I came here today not just to apologize to you but also to thank you. To thank you for waking me up, so to speak. I hope that you don't hate me."

"No, Jonathan, of course I don't hate you. I think it's very brave of you... what you said. I hope you continue to paint and I wish you all the very best," I say, struggling for my words.

"Thank you," he says earnestly as he walks to the door. "And thank you for hearing me out."

"Of course," I say as he opens the door to let himself out.

"Wow," I say out loud as I go to get my coffee; talk of coming out of left field. If that guy had money I'm convinced that there's not a woman in the world that could resist him. I look at the flowers and the chocolates that he left behind and decide that I should not accept them but should trash them, instead.

When I pick up the box of chocolates I notice that it feels quite heavy and, when I take a closer look, I'm realizing that it's not a box of chocolates, after all.

When I open up the box and take out the contents (which is wrapped in pink tissue paper), my eyes freeze. It's a recently painted portrait... of me. Even though I'm sure that he didn't have a photo of me to work from, the likeness, as far as I can be a judge is remarkable. It's clear that he didn't merely whip it up by throwing a few colors together; you can tell from the detail and the brush strokes that he really did take care with the painting.

Not only did he get the likeness correct but he also seems to have captured my personality or the essence of what makes me, me. As I turn it over I can see one word written in cursive on the back: Frances.

Having had such a fantastic time with Martin... I feel guilty holding this painting in my hands and I'm not sure what I should do and I don't even know what I'm feeling right at this moment. I feel like I just got emotionally blind-sided and everything is up in the air, all over again. What is it with me and younger men?

I should definitely not panic and I should probably give myself time to let my emotions settle... You know what? To heck with it, this painting and the roses are getting dumped and my heart belongs to Martin. I'm sure that things may change — as they usually do — but right now, Martin and I are an item and I'm not letting anything or anyone try to come between us.

If life has something else in store for me, then so be it, but for now, that is the way things stand. If my destiny lies here in LA or up north in San Rafael, then I'm sure that my path will become apparent as time moves on. Let's just see how everything goes, I guess.

I dump the roses and the painting in the trash and then sit down to relax and really enjoy my coffee. I love the change that is happening inside of me, as well as in my life and I pick up a pen and notepad to make some "to do" lists for the coming week.

I feel like I'm in some kind of weird and wonderful life flow and after I take a quick shower, I have a light lunch. I do some drawings for fun and then take a nap. In my light sleep, I'm having the most amazing dream. It's mostly a feeling dream, the kind where you don't really see people, or even know exactly what's happening, you just feel wonderful… and I do. In the dream I'm happy, like a balloon floating upward, higher and higher in the sky. Then I hear music from far away and I know that I have to come down to earth…

In the dream I realize that the music is *Good Vibrations* and when I open my eyes I can see that my cell phone is ringing. In a hazy, dreamy, almost-waking state, I feel a surge of joy and almost fall off the bed attempting to grab my phone because I know that it's Martin on the other end. "Hello sweetness," I answer his call. "Do you miss me?"

"I miss you so much, I can't help smiling," he says, sounding like he has a big grin on his face.

"I thought you were going to say that you miss me so much, it hurts. Why are you smiling?" I ask.

"I'm smiling because I've never before felt such pain over missing someone so much as I miss you."

"Oh, you charmer," I say, loving it.

"I'm smiling because I know that as soon as I get to be in your arms again, that pain will melt away and deep and lasting love will take its place."

"Are you on your way home? You better be really getting close to being here if you're going to talk poetry to me like that because I don't think I can wait any longer to have you in my arms again. Tell me you're on your way home."

"I'm standing on your porch," he says softly, "which is the purpose of my call. How soon can you let me in?"

"I'm letting you in now," I tell him as I glide my body to open the door. "I'm letting you in now."

ABOUT THE AUTHOR

Dermot is an Irish writer now living in the US. As a playwright, Dermot is a recipient of the O.Z. Whitehead Award which was co-sponsored by Irish Pen and the Society of Irish Playwrights. A fictional account of a dream therapist who is stuck in a dream from which he cannot awaken, with his debut novel, ""Stormy Weather," novelist Dermot Davis has deftly crafted a minor literary masterpiece," (Midwest Book Review).

His second novel, "Zen and Sex," is a witty and ironic first-person look at love and relationships as seen from the confused eyes of twenty-four-year old Martin who falls in love with Frances, a woman fourteen years his senior. Winner of two indie author awards and perhaps because it provides a no-holds-barred look into the mind of a man and his uncensored thoughts, it was suggested by the Kindle Book Review that, "every woman should read it as marriage counseling."

Winner of the 2013 USA Best Book Awards for humor, Dermot's third novel, "Brain: The Man That Wrote the Book That Changed the World," is "an entertaining farce about modern society; a deft, fast-paced tale that will leave self-aware readers giggling," (Publishers Weekly, starred review). Coming "Highly Recommended" by the Midwest Book Review, who also called it, "ironic, iconoclastic and pure entertainment from first page to last," the book poses the question of whether an author should write from the heart or write only books that he thinks will sell. I suspect that this novelist is trying to do both...

OTHER BOOKS BY DERMOT DAVIS

Stormy Weather

Zen and Sex

Brain: The Man Who Wrote the Book That Changed the World

7183454R00131

Printed in Great Britain
by Amazon.co.uk, Ltd.,
Marston Gate.